Vanessa Curtis

ZeLaH GReen

One More
Little Problem

EGMONT

EGMONT

We bring stories to life

Zelah Green: One More Little Problem first published in
Great Britain 2010
by Egmont UK Limited
239 Kensington High Street
London W8 6SA

Copyright © Vanessa Curtis 2010

The moral rights of the author have been asserted

ISBN 978 1 4052 4054 3

1 3 5 7 9 10 8 6 4 2

A CIP catalogue record for this title is available from
the British Library

Typeset by Avon DataSet Ltd, Bidford on Avon, Warwickshire
Printed and bound in Great Britain by the CPI Group

To Margaret, a true friend

Chapter One

My name's Zelah Green and I'm a Cleanaholic.

I'm upstairs in my bedroom dreaming about a boy I used to know. His name was Sol and although I only knew him for four weeks he's kind of got into my head and I can't get him out again.

I'm also trying to plan my summer break.

Most kids are going to Disney World or camping in the New Forest or jetting off to Australia.

My summer plans take the form of a list. This is what it says:

Clean the house from top to bottom.

Disinfect bathroom. (I have this little problem with something called OCD. It means that I hate germs and dirt.)

Scrub mud out of doormats and carpets.

Persuade Dad to have haircut.

Hide all alcohol in house in case Dad has a weak moment.

Cook and batch-freeze summer vegetables from garden.

Bake a cake.

Boring! When I read this list back I feel about ninety. What has happened to my carefree teenaged existence?

Oh yes – it all ended when my mother died, my stepmother tried to get rid of me, my father became a booze-soaked depressive, my best friend deserted me, I ended up in a treatment centre and my, erm, little problem got a bit out of control.

Put like that, the prospect of baking a cake doesn't seem too bad after all.

I'm measuring out some nice clean flour from a lovely sealed packet on to the disinfected white scales when Heather pops her head round the back door. Heather's our next-door neighbour and she's gorgeous. Oh, and she's also Dad's girlfriend, believe it or not.

'Mmm,' she says. 'Victoria sponge?'

I give her a scathing look.

'Purlease,' I say. 'You know full well that a Victoria sponge would involve the use of jam.'

I don't do jam. Horrid sticky smelly gloopy stuff clinging to the door handle of the fridge first thing in the morning. Major *Dirt Alert.*

I know. I'm a nightmare to live with.

'Fruitcake, then?' says Heather. She's in a very good mood this morning. Her sunglasses are in their usual place on top of her long shiny

hair and her face is glowing with sun and health. Unlike Dad, Heather is a big fan of eating five portions of fruit and veg a day.

'Heather,' I say. 'I'm disappointed in you. You're supposed to know me better than that. Fruitcake would involve the use of – *sultanas.*'

I shudder just using the word. I'm the only person I know who is scared of sultanas.

Heather gives a big sigh with her hands on her hips.

'I give up,' she says. 'Tell me, Zelah. Tell me what sort of cake you're making. Tell me before I go insane from not knowing.'

'Lemon,' I say, ignoring her sarcasm and gesturing at the lovely clean little bottle of lemon juice next to my mixing bowl.

Heather mock-slaps her forehead.

'Of course,' she says. 'Lemon. A perfect cleaning aid.'

I grin with pleasure. In fact I've already cleaned out the fridge today with a mixture of bicarbonate of soda and lemon juice and half a real lemon is sitting on the top shelf and soaking up all the vile old-meat-and-fish smells.

Lemons are big friends of mine. Kind of weird, I know, but as my real friends are a bit thin on the ground right now I need all the help I can get.

I did have a best friend – Fran – but she visited me when I was an inpatient at Forest Hill and she didn't Get It. She thought that if you were in any sort of hospital you must be totally bonkers.

But all that stuff seems pretty normal to me. My father is mad, after all, and although my mum's dead she was also crazy. Heather's not exactly Miss Sanest Person on the Planet either. She's not an out-and-out lunatic but you only have to spy on her doing ChiBall through

the lounge window to realise that she's kind of – unusual.

That's why Fran was so great. She comes from a very average sort of family. Her mother likes horses, *Country Living* magazine and filling up little French dishes with tiny fig-scented soaps. Her father is a mild-mannered accountant with round black spectacles and a tendency to mutter. The bedrooms in their house are full of plump white linen pillows and pale pink sheets. Fran is neatness personified with her pink summer dresses and flip-flops, her perfect matching pedicures and her dark brown plait hanging exactly down the middle of her back like a well-trained horsetail.

She's also very, very clean.

'You're doing that faraway thing again, kiddo,' says Heather.

I break away from my Fran-induced reverie.

'Sorry,' I say. 'Miles away.'

I gesture towards the eggs.

Heather understands. She's good like that.

She cracks the eggs into a bowl and beats them up so that I don't have to handle the gunky shells. Then she tips it all into the bowl where I've mixed up flour and sugar.

'Could you do the butter too?' I say. Butter paper is seriously gross.

Heather cuts half a packet of butter into tiny squares and tips them into the mix.

I squirt in loads of lemon juice and then beat the whole thing into submission while Heather greases the edges of the cake tin with the butter paper.

When the cake mix is poured into the tin and placed in the (very clean) oven, Heather asks where Dad is.

'Outside, where else?' I say.

Dad is at the end of the back garden clipping branches in half for a bonfire.

He's got his usual array of petrol cans, fish slices, scissors, tongs and rolled-up bits of newspaper, trying to start a fire.

We watch as Dad hops backwards when a flame shoots up and misses his eyebrows by about a millimetre and then dies away leaving a miserable stream of thin grey smoke behind.

Dad scratches his head and bumps his elbow on the tree behind him, trips up, falls over into a pile of compost and gets up again, brushing himself free of old tea bags and carrot tops.

Heather and I survey this sad spectacle in silence.

'You've got to love him, haven't you?' she says, after a while.

'Somebody has to,' I agree.

Heather bangs on the window and yells at Dad to come in.

Ha! If only it were that simple.

As he starts to come in through the kitchen door I call out to him just in time.

'Change outside,' I say. 'Sorry. It's just that smoke is major *Dirt Alert*.'

Dad makes a sort of growling noise and backs out into the garden, whipping off his shirt to reveal a nice eyeful of flabby middle-aged stomach, sprouting underarm hair and baggy old boxer shorts.

'Hands!' I shout through the window.

Dad washes his hands and hair under the outside tap.

'Shoes!' I yell.

Dad changes his cracked brown gardening shoes to indoor ones.

You might think this is a bit over the top. But I used to be far worse. Before Forest Hill

I wouldn't have let him inside the house at all.

When Dad finally gets back into the kitchen Heather dangles a bunch of keys in front of his bleary eyes.

'You're in charge of my house,' she says.

Dad scratches his head.

'What on earth for?' he says.

Heather gives a small puff of frustration.

'PATRICK!' she says. 'I'm off to Slovenia, remember? You're to water my plants? And Zelah, you can use my laptop if you like.'

Heather knows that Dad's computer is slow and can only do one thing at a time. I have an Atari games thing from the 1970s that Dad picked out of a skip but it only has three games on it and they didn't have the Internet in the olden days.

Dad glances outside into the street where Heather's red Porsche contains a couple of

suitcases and some expensive leather hand luggage.

'Oh. You're going now, are you?' is all he says.

'You know I am,' she says. 'We've discussed all this, Patrick. Remember?'

Dad picks at some dirt behind his fingernails.

I keep a close eye on where he puts the specks of earth.

Heather is fluffing up her hair in the kitchen mirror and checking her eyeliner.

Then she kisses Dad and air-kisses me.

'Keep an eye on your dad, Zelah,' she says. 'I trust you. You'll be fine. And if you need me, I'm on the end of the mobile. OK, kiddo?'

I nod in a sad sort of way. It won't be the same without Heather around. She's kind of like my replacement mum.

Then she's slamming our front door and

bounding off towards the car, sliding her pencil-thin frame into the front seat and roaring off into the Slovenian sunset.

Dad and I look at each other over the huge bunch of keys.

'Might as well go next door and see what's what,' he mumbles.

We head up Heather's neat front path. Her garden looks like the 'after' version of ours. Ours is very definitely 'before'.

I look back over the fence at our mangled overgrown wilderness of a front garden with the old broken sofa and the ancient toilet bowl with ivy growing around the base. Dad seems to have forgotten all about the front garden. Mum used to keep the front nice with pots on little feet sprouting pink and red flowers and miniature daffodils poking through squares of coloured paving.

I mentally add another chore to my ever-

growing summer list of fun things to do:

Make front garden look tidy.

Then we step into the paradise which is Heather's house next door.

Chapter Two

The really weird thing about Heather's house is that on the outside it is exactly the same as ours, but on the inside it's like stepping into a different country, or even a different world.

Long polished corridors with wooden floors stretch towards a huge glass kitchen extension at the back of the house. Heather had this put in when she got a big cash bonus for being Fashion Editor of the Year. The kitchen is full of gorgeous big pieces of pottery and artfully placed green tropical plants with leaves that droop at just the right

angle from the windowsills. The floor is made from cool grey slate tiles and the ceiling is inset with tiny round spotlights that shine a pure white light down on to the granite kitchen work surfaces.

The walls in Heather's house are all the most pristine white. Here and there is a minimalist piece of modern art showing a blaze of orange or a calm sweep of Mediterranean blue against the white. But mostly it's all just – white.

I love the white. Most of all I love that the house is so clean.

Heather pays Tina-the-Cleaner to come in three times a week and keep her house looking the way she likes it.

If Dad wasn't unemployed I think I'd ask Tina to come and sort our house out too, but I reckon we can't afford it. Plus she might well get lost underneath the piles of decaying crappy furniture and old carpets. And she

smokes, and although Heather has banned her from lighting up inside, my dad would just smile and let her smoke herself to death in the living room.

In Heather's house I don't have to tuck my elbows into my sides or hold my breath as I walk down the hallway or up the stairs. There are no grimy smears on the oak banisters or bits of dried snot on the walls or rancid smells of food past its sell-by date.

I'd quite like to move in with Heather but she's always going on about how she isn't very maternal.

Shame. If I moved in with Heather there's just the smallest chance that my little problem might get better.

Or even go away.

Dad's not interested in Heather's house. He splashes some water on a few house plants

even though she's only just watered them and then slopes off home to his asparagus beds.

I rescue the drowning plants and then go into Heather's shiny disinfected kitchen to lean back against her gleaming black Aga.

I take a deep breath of all my favourite smells: bleach, apple-scented washing-up liquid and lemony dishwasher tablets.

We don't have those smells at home.

Hey! I could use Heather's new laptop to surf the Internet and check my email. Dad's computer is so ancient that it takes half an hour to download even the most basic website.

But computer keyboards are evil.

I read that they have more germs in them than an entire toilet.

Keyboards are like major *Germ Alert* AND *Dirt Alert* all at once.

I pull on a brand new pair of pink rubber

gloves from the pile kept by Heather's cleaner, grab a new bottle of disinfectant spray and head to the office.

I roll the gloves as high up my arms as possible and then pick up Heather's keyboard by the tips of my fingers and shake it upside down with a shudder.

A little spray of crumbs, dust and bent paperclips hits the desk.

Gross.

I sweep all the gunk into the bin and then give the computer keyboard a good scrubbing with the disinfectant before shaking it upside down again one more time just to check I've got every life-threatening germ out of there.

Then I settle down, log on to the net and am just about to start surfing about a bit when I notice that Heather's stuck a little yellow post-it note on the desk next to the laptop.

'Zelah, friend of mine's just launched this

site,' it says. 'Might be fun to give it a try? Hx.'

There's a website address so I type it into the search engine and watch while a pink website flashing big red hearts pops up on Heather's screen.

'Aged fourteen to sixteen? Register now for fun, friendship and flirting at *mysortaspace*, the site everyone's talking about,' it says.

I roll my eyes and slump back in the chair.

Yuk!

But then I think about the fact that the one boy I really like, I'll probably never see again and then I think about the prospect of yet another evening with Dad being gloomy and I don't know what comes over me but I click on the link and before I know it I've set myself up a profile on *mysortaspace.com* and registered to get a password.

My new secret dating name isn't very imaginative. I just call myself 'Zelah'.

And I'm not putting a photo on there.

My face is all red-raw from a mad bout of scrubbing last night and my hair has stopped being sleek and swishy and grown back into mad black fuzz since the haircut from Forest Hill.

An email flashes into my new inbox, welcoming me to the website and telling me that any interested flirty boys can now send me emails in confidence.

I sink into my chair and bury my face in my hands.

What am I doing? Even if I did meet the boy of my dreams I wouldn't actually be able to touch him so you can imagine the fun date that we'd have, waving at one another from opposite sides of the sofa that might as well be opposite sides of the planet.

Plus boys don't actually wash much so there's a risk of major *Dirt Alert* AND

Germ Alert if I ever meet up with one.

And there's another thing. I already met the boy of my dreams three months ago.

He had olive skin and dark hair and scowling brown eyes.

Oh Sol. I miss you. Loads.

I switch everything off and lock the office before staggering back next door for a comforting Ribena and a stale custard cream.

It's only the second day of the summer holidays and already my little problem has flared up a bit after the madness of signing on with *mysortaspace.com*.

So I'm doing thirty-one jumps on the bottom stair just to make myself feel a bit better.

I used to do hundreds of jumps but after a lot of help I managed to cut them down to fifteen a day. At the moment I'm doing at least

thirty on the bottom step and the same on the top and then the whole thing in reverse when I come down again.

I'm just in the process of doing the final few jumps when the doorbell rings.

Damn.

Dad's down the bottom of the garden with a big fork in his hand. I can't answer the door until I've finished the ritual or else lots of bad things might happen (although you could say they already have, seeing as my mother is dead, my father is unemployed, my neighbour's bogged off to a foreign land and my ex-best friend thinks that I am a deranged lunatic, which I probably am seeing as how I'm standing on the staircase jumping up and down in broad daylight).

I finish as fast as I can, aware that whoever is on the other side of the frosted glass front door can see my shadow leaping about.

Well, I'll just have to pretend I was head-banging to thrash metal or something.

I finish my jumps off, tidy my frizzy black hair in the hall mirror and approach the front door.

There's something familiar about the small slouching shadow on the other side of the glass.

Doesn't look like the postman. He's tall and ginger.

I pull open the door and then I nearly fall over in shock.

Tiny frame, long fair hair dipping over her tired face, dark circles underneath her huge eyes and the usual black outfit of baggy trousers, biker boots, armbands and T-shirt with the white moony face of a satanic death-metal singer staring out at me.

'Well, aren't you going to ask me in, OCD?' says the small girl. 'Jeez. I've come about two

hundred miles to visit you. You could look a bit more pleased.'

She pushes past me.

I stand for a moment on the front doorstep trying to pull my shattered thoughts back into order.

Then I close my gaping mouth and follow her into the house.

Chapter Three

Caro. The girl who made my time at Forest Hill House either a complete and utter nightmare or, sometimes, a bit of a relief. There was never much in between.

Forest Hill. The place I was sent to three months ago when my stepmother decided she couldn't cope with my rituals any longer.

I'd heard from some of the other kids at Forest Hill House, but not Caro.

I'd kind of missed her but now she's sitting in my kitchen with that weird look on her face – half-grumpy, half-defiant with a micro-speck of shyness hidden somewhere underneath –

I remember how much air she seems to suck up. And how many grey vibes of angst she can puff out into the atmosphere without even speaking.

Caro can change the mood of a room by just sitting down in it.

She can be very tiring.

I click the kettle on and look down the garden to where my father is spraying the leaves of a giant marrow plant with some weird mixture of milk and water that he insists gets rid of mould.

Caro follows my glance.

'Jeez, OCD,' she says. 'I know you're posh and all that, but I never knew you had a gardener.'

My back prickles with indignation and I'm about to stand up for Dad, but then I look out again and see him through a stranger's eyes and I feel embarrassed and confused and too

tired to bother explaining. In his old brown apron and worn-down shoes with grotty gloves and a weird flat cap, he does look a bit like a sad old gardener.

'Yeah,' is all I say. 'He's good with vegetables. Coffee? Tea? Hell's Juice?'

Caro does her small cheek-twitch smile, the one where it looks as if a baby moth has landed on her face and she's trying half-heartedly to remove it.

'Coffee,' she says. 'Black. Obviously. Is there any other colour?'

I give her a cautious smile back. She fiddles with her fingernails, the black leather wristbands on her thin arms sliding up and down.

'How've you been?' I say, spooning evil black granules into a mug. Dad drinks a lot of rubbish instant coffee. Heather is forever trying to hide the jar and force him to drink The Proper Stuff, as she calls it. She makes this

in a large shiny pot from some designer kitchen store, and serves it in giant white ceramic cups with tiny flowers on them and little caramel biscuits in nice sanitised plastic placed on the side of the saucer.

I plonk a cracked mug and half a packet of stale Bourbons next to Caro.

'Cheers, Big Ears,' she says, rolling up a cigarette and putting her heavy-duty black boots up on the edge of my chair.

She tips her seat back and takes a long drag from the fag, blowing smoke up into the air.

I duck. Major *Dirt Alert*!

Caro smirks.

'Still got your funny little habits then, OCD?' she says. 'Saw you jumping on the stairs just now. Figured you might have cut out all that rubbish.'

'And have you stopped cutting yourself?' I shoot back. Caro really is winding me up.

She's taken over the kitchen, eaten five biscuits in three seconds and is polluting the air around my head.

Caro's smile fades a little and she tugs at her sleeves to hide her wrists.

There's no need. The sleeves are already down to her fingertips, covering up her arms.

'Dunno, really,' she mutters.

Typical Caro. I mean – she must KNOW if she's cutting herself or not. Unless she's possessed by the spirit of Marilyn Manson while she's doing it and enters some sort of trance. Which I doubt. Because you have to be dead to become a spirit, right? And Manson's not dead.

I rescue the last biscuit, check it for cigarette ash and pop it into my mouth.

'I take it that you're still cutting, then?' I say.

My voice sounds harsh and unfeeling. I'm ashamed. Maybe she has come an awful long

way to see me. Her angelic face is etched with tiredness and there are the usual mauve shadows underneath her eyes.

Caro breathes out a quivering smoke ring above our heads and stubs her limp cigarette on the biscuit plate.

I remove the plate with my fingertips and dump it in the sink at arm's length.

I catch her eye.

The tension in the room hovers, evaporates, and then we're both laughing.

Proper laughs.

'Look at us,' says Caro. 'You couldn't make us up, could you?'

I tell Caro about Heather and my dad's unemployment and how I've managed to cut down some of my rituals since I last saw her.

She gives me an appraising stare.

'Yeah,' she says. 'You look more relaxed. At Forest Hill you were always jumping up and

washing the whole time. Or thinking about washing.'

I'm just basking in the glow of this rare compliment when she does another typical Caro thing by following it with a dazzling insult.

'You're fatter though,' she says.

I'm not going to let her get to me.

'Perhaps I could say the same to you,' I say.

We both know that Caro is about as far from fat as it's possible to be. She's got to be at least a Size Zero. And even then there was a girl at Forest Hill who made Caro look obese in comparison.

'OK, OCD,' Caro says, holding up her hands in mock-defence. 'Chillax! I touched a nerve there!'

I sneak a look at my watch. It's gone lunchtime and Dad will come in at any moment to make himself a limp cheese sandwich and a

can of lager, his usual I'm-unemployed-can't-be-bothered-oh-woe-is-me sort of meal.

'Look, I don't mean to be rude,' I begin, 'and it's great to see you, it really is. But — erm, how long are you planning on staying?'

Caro tips some worm-like shreds of tobacco out of a green pouch and starts to roll up another cigarette. It's like she exists in a different time zone to everyone else. A zone where time doesn't exist.

'Might hang out here for a while,' she says, all casual. 'Not getting on very well with my olds. My foster olds, that is. Had a huge ruck last night and I kind of walked out on them.'

'How did you get here from Somerset?' I say. 'Where did you spend the night then?'

'Lorry,' says Caro. 'Hitched a ride with some old dude delivering boxes of underwear to London. Made a pillow out of knickers and kipped in the back.'

As ever, Caro leaves me floundering like a small lost fish in a big rough sea.

Just as I'm wondering what on earth to say to this, Dad slopes into the kitchen, casts a brief look at Caro, ferrets around for white bread and starts slicing up some dubious green-mould Cheddar.

'Yes please, gardener man,' says Caro. 'Got any pickle?'

I nearly fall off my chair.

My dad chuckles, a rare and much-missed sound. He gets some extra bread out of the packet and produces a jar of rancid chutney from behind a row of out-of-date Pot Noodles.

'I don't know who you are,' he says. 'But it's about time people said what they felt. Too many people dither about all around the houses. I like a girl with attitude.'

I'm even more shocked.

'This is Caro,' I say in my prim voice. I'm eyeing up the butter-laden knife with distaste. Butter and I have a long historical relationship of mistrust.

'You know – *Caro*?' I try again. 'We were at Forest Hill together? I might have told you about her?'

My father turns round and sizes Caro up with renewed interest.

'Oh yes,' he says. 'You're the one who slices yourself to bits. Interesting hobby. Can't you find something less dramatic – acting classes or whatever?'

I nearly pass out with embarrassment and fear. Fear of what Caro might do or say to this astonishing remark. But to my surprise Caro laughs and pushes her packet of worms towards Dad.

'Smoke?' she says.

Dad nods and rolls one up, even though he

hasn't smoked roll-ups since about 1980.

'Your gardener's OK for an old bloke,' she says to me, chomping down on the sandwich as if the packet of biscuits was a phantom snack.

'Her gardener is in fact her father,' says Dad. 'But I take it as a compliment from one so young and bitter.'

'Ah,' says Caro. 'So you're the old dude who pays the mortgage here. Right?'

Dad nods.

'In that case,' she says, 'I need to ask you if I can stay. For about six weeks. As much free tobacco and verbal abuse as you can handle.'

Dad screws up his mouth on one side. I can see he's trying not to laugh.

'Can you cook?' he asks.

Both Caro and I laugh at this one.

'No she sodding well can't,' I splutter.

'Clean?' says Dad.

Caro raises one scornful pierced eyebrow and says, 'Pur-lease!'

'Got any money for rent?' says Dad. I swear he's enjoying this. I haven't seen his eyes spark up in that way for quite some time.

'Nope, skint as a badger,' says Caro.

'And do you get on with my daughter?' says Dad. 'That's the all-important question.'

At last! He's showing some signs of fatherly protectiveness. I heave a quiet sigh of relief. I mean – I do like Caro in small doses and all that, but the thought of having her here the entire summer while I try to clean the house and get Dad to his interviews on time . . .

'OCD?' Caro is saying. 'Yeah. She's all right. Bit demented with all the jumping and stuff.'

'Tell me about it,' says Dad. 'But that's my Princess. That's Zelah.'

Gee, thanks, Dad.

I go over to the sink to wash up. I'm in

shock. This day is getting weirder and weirder.

Just as I start running the taps I turn around to see Dad and Caro shaking hands.

'Deal?' she says.

'Deal,' says Dad. 'Welcome to our crazy house of love.'

With that, my entire summer falls about my ears.

And crashes to the floor.

Chapter Four

There's a small ray of hope when Dad rings up Caro's foster parents to ask whether they mind her staying with us.

Turns out they're not best pleased about her hiking down the motorway without telling them.

I'm upstairs listening on the extension and keeping my fingers crossed so tight that the blood flow is cut off and my knuckles are all white and transparent.

Honestly – I love Caro, but even living in the room next door to her for a month at Forest Hill nearly finished me off. Caro's not

the type to sit down and read a book or watch a good DVD. Either she's blasting out her satanic rock metal CDs at top volume or she's in a screaming mood, banging doors and smashing glasses on tables and hurling abuse at authority figures.

And then there's all that blood.

Blood and OCD are a vile combination. Blood is *Dirt Alert* AND *Germ Alert*.

It's bad enough that I've got to put up with Caro all summer without having to mop up her blood too.

The thought of it makes me come over funny and I drop the phone on the bed for a moment.

Dad's voice booms out of the receiver.

'She'd be no trouble at all,' he's saying. 'It would be a pleasure. Any friend of Zelah's is welcome in my house.'

I come over all funny for a second time.

I've never thought of Caro as a friend, exactly.

She couldn't be less like Fran if she tried.

I'm tempted to pick up the phone and shout something desperate to try and stop the whole horrid blood-soaked nightmare from beginning. But Dad would be angry and I feel too tired to cope with that. Although in some ways, his anger is easier to deal with than this new I-love-everybody sort of Dad.

'OK,' says a high female voice. I presume that this must be Caro's foster mother. From the way that Caro used to describe her you'd think she was the Spawn of the Devil. Instead she sounds soft and mild and worn out.

'I suppose it would be nice to have a bit of a break from her,' says the tired voice. 'She's a good girl at heart but can be a little – well, demanding.'

Dad gives a friendly chuckle.

'You don't need to tell me about having a

demanding daughter,' he says. 'Believe me – I know!'

I slam the phone down. Don't care if he's heard me now. This is beyond a joke. Me? Difficult? I am an angel child compared to Caro!

'Zelah!' Dad shouts up the stairs. 'It's very rude to listen to people's conversations on the phone.'

I pretend not to hear.

I go downstairs to see what Caro is up to.

She's plugged into her iPod and has her biker boots up on the kitchen table while her head sways in a sort of corpse-like trance to the hideous sounds of Marilyn Manson.

I push her legs on to the floor.

'OK, chill, OCD,' she snarls. 'Few bits of dirt won't kill you.'

I sit down next to Caro and watch her head-bang for a moment.

Is this how my entire summer is going to be? Me trying to be polite and her ignoring me and tainting my nice clean surfaces with smoke, blood and cigarette ash?

'What are you listening to?' I yell, in a bid to restart conversation.

Caro unhooks one earpiece and inserts it into my ear.

I remove it – major *Dirt Alert* – wipe it and hold it just outside my eardrum.

Manson is growling and muttering his way through a 'song' with a demonic-sounding guitar repeating the same jerky riff underneath. The 'song', according to the little screen on the iPod, is called 'The Beautiful People'.

'Yeah. It's – good,' I offer. I pass the earpiece back to her and wipe my hands with a shudder.

Caro snorts.

'You're a rubbish liar, OCD,' she says.

'You always were. Like when you pretended that you didn't fancy Sol.'

I flush a horrid hot crimson. Sol was the only boy resident at Forest Hill House during my month-long stay. He never spoke because watching his father run over his mother had traumatised him. It was just an everyday story of family murder in the streets of South London.

We kind of clicked.

But then Dad came and found me at Forest Hill and in the excitement of seeing him I kind of forgot about Sol and when I left the house for good he'd gone back to South London with his father to try and start a new life.

'See,' Caro is saying. 'Even just thinking about him you've gone all moony and pathetic.'

I clear my throat and get up from the table.

Chapter Five

The phone rings later on when Caro, Dad and I are sitting around the kitchen table eating miniature Brussels sprouts on toast.

The sprouts are not supposed to have been picked until Christmas but something went wrong and Dad had to cut them off their stalks three months early.

'Thank God,' I mutter as the insistent ringing coming from the hallway gives me a chance to abandon both the hideous food and the weird conversation my father is having with Caro – something about legal versus illegal tobacco. Great.

'Hi, kiddo,' says a familiar voice on a crackly mobile phone. 'How's everything going?'

At the sound of Heather's voice something unexpected happens. I well up with pathetic girlie tears, even though she's not my real mum. Heather kind of gets *Dirt Alert* and *Germ Alert* and I feel as if we've got An Understanding. Plus she's all adult and not moody, unlike most people in my life.

And now she's trusted me to look after Dad and catch up on my schoolwork and this isn't exactly happening the way she planned it.

Do I tell her?

'Dad really misses you,' I start (true), 'and I really miss you as well,' (also true), 'and I'm doing loads of homework,' (complete lie).

Heather says 'Oh, good!'

In the background are lots of clinking and splashing noises.

'Sorry kiddo,' she yells over the noise.

'Champagne poolside party. You know how it is! But tell me what else you're up to?'

My mouth kind of freezes half-open when she says this.

I don't know where to begin.

'I'm fine,' I manage. 'I'm having a great summer holiday.'

I feel tears welling up again at this reference to some mystical faraway paradise that I can only dream of, so I grab a clean tissue to stop them in their germy little tracks.

I want to tell Heather about Caro turning up and Dad going weird. And I really, really want to tell her about the website I've just registered on and my fears about Boys.

But I don't.

I just go: 'Have a lovely time. Thanks for ringing, I'll get Dad,' in the voice of a strangled chicken and I put down the phone and get Dad.

I go and sit in the front garden and have a big snivelling cry.

After the cry I feel better. I get the shears out of the shed and trim what's left of the orange geraniums to exactly the same height. I'm kind of embarrassed to be doing this but I like things to be neat and tidy.

Not much hope of that inside the kitchen.

Caro and Dad are rolling cigarettes and sharing a can of beer. Dirty plates cover the table and all the work surfaces. Dad has taken off his mouldy work boots and is sitting in muddy grey socks. Caro's got her black biker boots on the table again. The air is full of raucous laughter and stale smoke.

For the first time in ages I miss Fran.

I mean, she said some vile things that last time I saw her but at least you could rely on her to be clean and smell like a fragrant summer's day. Fran would have washed up her

dirty plates and wiped the table down and swept the floor.

I wash up the dirty plates, wipe the table down and sweep the floor.

Then I leave them speaking the language of the devil and go upstairs to scrub my face.

Next day's Tuesday.

I wake up with a sinking kind of feeling. Judging by the loud snores coming from across the landing, Dad isn't going to be in the best of states to go and start job-hunting even though he promised Heather he would on the phone last night.

I get up and switch on my CD player. At the moment I'm listening to 'American Idiot' by Green Day. I load up a scrubbing brush with soap to do my rituals.

This is what I do:

Twenty scrubs of my right cheek.

Twenty scrubs of my left cheek.

Ten scrubs of my right hand.

Ten scrubs of my left hand.

Then I brush my frizzy black hair twenty-five times in total, tie it into a neat pony, slide into my clean cut-off jeans and silver flip-flops and select a nice calming blue vest top from my wardrobe where all the clothes hang at equal distances with exactly the same gaps in between them.

I used to have a ruler to do this but the Doc helped me stop that. Now I just judge the distance by standing back and gazing at the clothes with a critical eye.

I move a blue dress about a half a centimetre to the left and a flippy long white skirt about three centimetres to the right.

There.

Perfect.

Now that I've done my bedroom and

bathroom rituals there's only one set left to do.

The stairs.

I do thirty-one jumps on the top step and thirty-one on the bottom so that I can head into the kitchen and relax.

Did I say 'relax'?

The sight that greets me as I enter fails to encourage a sense of relaxation.

Dad and Caro must have stayed up chatting half the night because when I went to bed the kitchen was cleaned to perfection (by me) and now there are cans, bottles, ashtrays, chocolate wrappers and CDs littered all over the wooden table, the chairs and the floor.

Oh well. At least there's nobody in here yet. Maybe I can have a good think about dating and boys and, gulp, Sol while I'm washing up.

I twiddle the knob on the radio until I find Radio One and then I slide a pair of nice clean yellow rubber gloves right up my arms and

poke around in the plughole with a shudder to remove something that looks like a clump of hair in gravy tied up with some green seaweed and then I scrub the stainless steel sink until it shines my hot reflection back at me and then I set to on the rest of the kitchen with grim determination.

Dad staggers down about an hour later and swallows three painkillers straight off.

'She can hold her drink, that little friend of yours,' he says. He's grey in the face and looks about a hundred.

He fails to notice the clean sparkling kitchen.

'I could murder a fry-up, Princess,' he says.

I slam a box of oats and a jug of milk down in front of him.

'Oh yes, that's right,' says Dad, all mournful. 'You only eat rabbit food.'

He pours oats into a bowl and crunches

through them with a pained expression on his tired face.

I go into the hall to pick up the post.

There's an official-looking letter with Dad's name typed on the white envelope.

'Probably a bill,' he says as I hand it over.

Dad is chewing on a mouthful of oats but as he skim-reads the letter his cheek freezes into a hamster bulge and he drops his spoon with a loud clatter.

'I don't believe it,' he says. 'I seriously don't believe it!'

I go and stand behind his shoulder (without touching it, of course).

The letter is from the school board and seems to be inviting Dad to an interview.

'Dad!' I scream. 'That's fantastic! You've got an interview! At last!'

Dad gets up and we do a silly virtual hug-dance around in a circle, him with his grey

dressing gown flapping and me waving my arms about in the air.

Then as a special treat I fry him an egg at arm's length and covered in a full body apron just in case of grease splattering and it smells so tempting that I cave in and fry myself one as well and we stuff our faces and for a moment I forget all about Caro being upstairs.

Dad hasn't, though.

'Is your little friend gracing us with her presence today?' he says.

I laugh. Caro never did surface before lunchtime.

'Shame,' Dad says. He actually looks disappointed.

'Dad,' I say. 'It's really good that you and Caro are getting on so well but the thing is, I find her quite difficult to handle sometimes – I mean, she can have awful screaming fits and

she does that cutting stuff – I'm not sure if you realise . . .'

Dad gets up and clicks the kettle on.

'I realise,' he says. 'But I think she's charming.'

I nearly fall off my chair.

'Charming' is one word I would NOT apply to Caro. Irritating, temperamental, rude, aggressive, yes. But CHARMING?

'OK,' I mutter in a dark voice. 'But don't say I didn't warn you.'

Dad's gone. He's upstairs running the shower and whistling. I haven't heard him this cheerful in a long time.

I take a deep breath. Maybe things are looking up. Dad's happy and if he's happy, then that makes me happy as well.

I text Heather: 'Dad got interview! Zx' and she texts back 'Gr8!' straight away.

I feel a bit better then, better about

everything. Even the prospect of checking my new email account doesn't feel quite so bad now.

I mean – what could really be so scary about an email?

Right?

Chapter Six

It's three in the afternoon and I'm in Heather's office again. I've booked in a diary session with Caro later. I'm going to teach her how to clean the kitchen.

Dad's gone out to buy himself a new suit for the interview and to get a much-needed haircut.

With my heart flopping in big painful spasms I log into my new account on *mysortaspace.com*.

A little flashing box pops up next to a picture of a tiny yellow envelope.

You have one new message!

'What's the point?' I mutter to myself. 'It's not going to improve my life, is it?'

But there's something a bit thrilling about the little yellow envelope sitting there all mysterious and unopened.

My heart has only just calmed down again but now it leaps into my chest and starts up a slow painful thud that gathers pace into a crazy woodpecker rhythm.

'Calm, calm, phoo, phoo,' I go, taking deep breaths with my hand on my chest just like the Doc showed me at Forest Hill.

My heart slows down, but only a tiny bit.

I click into my inbox and there's an email with the heading 'Hi. Want to chat?'

'Not sure,' I mutter, but curiosity gets the better of me. I open up the message and begin to read.

'*Hi Zelah,*' says the mail. '*Wow what an unusual name! I had to write to you when I saw that name.*

But of course it's probably not your real name. I mean — nobody's called "Zelah". Right?

'Wrong,' I say in a huff. What's so bad about my name? Yes, it's unusual, but only because my dead mother got it out of a Cornish hiking magazine with her eyes shut and a stabbing pencil.

When the lead of that pencil touched the glossy page, a whole life of people blinking and saying 'Pardon?' and exclaiming at my unusual name lay ahead.

And I was only one week old.

I read my way down the email from the mystery flirting person.

He says his name is 'Alessandro' and that he plays in a heavy-metal band and the rest of the time studies for his GCSEs and plays football and goes to the gym.

Then he goes on a bit about the sort of

music he listens to and the TV programmes that he likes and I can feel my eyes glazing over a bit and then I get to the final line.

Oh, and my dad's in the slammer. But not for anything really bad like murder. Just for stealing stuff. You know, Zelah — the usual sorta thing.

I draw myself up into an indignant pillar.

No, I do not know!

My father might be many things — sarcastic, miserable and depressed just for starters — but he's never been in prison. Not as far as I know, anyway.

Great. The first reply I get and it has to be from some weirdo with an old man in jail.

I shut down my inbox and retreat back home in disgust with Heather's laptop under my arm so that I don't have to keep going next door to check it.

Little images of lovely Sol and his dark scowling sexy eyes keep getting in the way.

I come home all worn out to take a cleaning lesson with Caro.

'This green stuff is washing-up liquid,' I say.

'And this is a scourer, to get all the tricky stains off the cooker.'

'Yeah yeah,' says Caro. I'd say she's lost interest, but that would imply that she had some in the first place.

'Look,' I say, with an icy edge to my voice. 'If you're going to live here for six weeks rent-free, you've got to help me out. It's not fair.'

'Ooh, it's not fair! Poor little OCD!' mimics Caro in a high squeaky voice nothing like my own.

I hate being referred to as 'OCD'.

I take a deep 'phoo, phoo,' breath with my hand on my chest.

'Just get cleaning, please,' I say, putting the

scourer and liquid into her black-nailed hands.

Caro looks at them in disgust but goes over to the sink and does some half-hearted wiping with a fag hanging from her lips and an iPod stuffed into her eardrums.

I'm not in the mood for hearing the rasping satanic mutterings of Marilyn Manson so I go upstairs.

I sit on Mum's side of what used to be her and Dad's bed and I feel all hopeless and dried-up with exhaustion. Again.

I miss Mum. She was bonkers and told elaborate stories with not even one single grain of truth in them but she was very good at listening to what she called 'women's problems'.

Heather's good at all that stuff too. But she's not here.

I sigh and pat the bed.

'Miss you, Mum,' I say.

There's the faintest whiff of Miss Dior perfume in the air.

Mum's favourite. I often smell it when I'm sad.

Then I go downstairs to inspect Caro's cleaning.

Dad gets back from his quest to buy an interview suit clutching a purple carrier bag and with a smart new haircut.

My eyes fill up with big tears just looking at him.

'Dad,' I croak. 'You look like you used to.'

Dad looks worried.

'Is that a good or a bad thing?' he says, plonking his bag down and pulling out a lovely new grey suit for my inspection.

'It's good, deffo,' I say. 'You look kind of – younger. And less like a sad old hippie.'

Caro is peering at the suit.

'Jeez,' she says. 'Wouldn't catch me dead in something like that. And shame about the hair. I liked your old rock-guy look.'

Dad looks confused, anxious and pleased all at the same time.

I give Caro a sharp look.

'Don't put him off, please,' I hiss. 'We've been waiting a long time for this interview.'

'I'm just saying,' she growls.

'Well, don't,' I say. 'And the fridge needs cleaning out. Bicarb of soda and half a lemon.'

'When's tea break?' Caro is saying. 'I'm in need of sugar and alcohol.'

'When you've finished,' I say.

I'm turning into a right little taskmaster. But it's the only way with Caro. If you're nice to her, she walks all over you in her biker boots and makes you wish you'd never been born.

Or conceived.

Or even thought of.

'I've nearly finished, man,' says Caro. She looks so funny in her apron with rubber gloves on and a fag hanging out of her mouth that I can't help but smile at her.

'You're doing a good job,' I say, trying to make amends.

Caro grunts at this, but she gives me a half-hearted grin before turning back to our scummy sink.

I get Dad to try on his suit. It looks really smart. I can tell he's quite pleased with the way he looks because he keeps twisting and turning in front of the mirror, keeping an eye on his trendy new haircut and slimline silhouette.

Then I tell Caro to wash all the kitchen windows inside and out and am about to go upstairs and actually unpack my school homework from my bag where it's been festering since day one of the holidays when a text message pops up on my mobile.

'You have a message from Alessandro on *mysortaspace.com*!' it says. Yikes! I forgot I'd given them my mobile number when I registered.

I sink down on to the top step with a heavy sigh. If I peer towards my bedroom I can just see my school bag with a green geography exercise book poking out of one corner.

It seems that's about as close as I'm going to get to what I'm supposed to be doing this summer.

I could really do with some advice about whether or not to log on and reply to the new email.

And I feel a bit lonely with Heather away.

There's only one person who would be able to tell me what to do.

Only one person who knows all about flirting with boys even though she tosses her plaits and pretends to ignore them.

The problem is, that person is the only person I can't ask for anything ever again.

But I reckon I'm going to have to swallow a whole heap of pride along with my revolting vegetable dinner tonight.

I need to stop having this lonely holiday.

I need my best friend back.

I have to ring Fran.

Chapter Seven

I always thought that Fran and I would be friends forever. We'd even done one of those blood pact things where you cut your wrists and put them together but because of my little problem, Fran was the only one who actually touched the blood and it was her own, not mine.

Maybe that's where we went wrong. Maybe the pact should have involved my blood too. But blood is major *Germ Alert* AND *Dirt Alert*.

Since we broke up as friends I've tried not to think about Fran.

But it's easier said than done. I've been

round her house so many times that I can imagine every single thing she does, right from the moment when she wakes up on her pink pillow, checks her silver alarm clock and bounces out of bed to the moment when she climbs back up the cream-coloured stairs, cleans her teeth in the white bathroom with her yellow toothbrush and clicks off her soft pink reading light.

I picture all this stuff on a regular basis.

It's like comforting, but also torture.

Because I'm not part of that picture any more.

But that's all going to change.

Dad's already downstairs when I come down in my cut-off jeans, silver flip-flops and a pale blue T-shirt.

'You'll wear out that stair carpet with your jumping,' he says.

This is a very un-Dad-like comment. The Doc advised him not to draw attention to my rituals, as it would slow down my recovery.

He must be feeling nervous.

I sit him at the table and make him toast, slide the evil pot of jam in his direction and pour out large mugs of tea to calm our nerves.

It's only eight o'clock and Caro won't be up until lunchtime so it's just the two of us sitting over breakfast.

It feels good. Dad's got the new suit on and has washed his short hair and punked up the front with some gel. He's added some little black-rimmed teacher glasses to complete the look.

The man in front of me is almost unrecognisable from the check-shirted hunchbacked digging gardener with the grubby nails.

I take a photo on my mobile and send it to Heather. She's always saying to me that she

loves Dad for who he is but that he could do with smartening up a bit (understatement).

Besides which it's quite stressful for a person with my little problem to have a dirty smelly father.

Today Dad smells of pine shampoo and citrus shaving gel.

A message flashes back on my mobile.

'Who is handsome man? Hx'

I don't know whether she's joking, or whether she thinks I'm having breakfast with a complete stranger.

'She's joking,' says Dad, reading the message over my shoulder and trying not to give a pleased smirk.

I wait until he's brushed his teeth and picked up his briefcase and driven off to his interview.

Then I do some extra jumps on the stairs and a good forty or so face washes upstairs in the bathroom.

I brush my hair until it crackles with static and sticks up in the air.

Then I tie it up with a blue ribbon and find some long blue sparkly earrings.

This is all really annoying but I need to get myself prepared for what I have to do next.

I can still remember the number off by heart.

I creep into Dad's room and shut the door. Don't want Caro hearing any of this.

I sit on the Mum side of the bed.

I take a deep 'phoo, phoo,' breath with my hand on my chest.

And then I dial Fran.

Chapter Eight

Fran's mother answers the phone in a yummy-mummy voice.

'Good morning, Fenella Benson speaking?'

This throws me into a complete panic.

'Erm, hello, Mrs Benson,' I start.

Then I stop.

Fran's probably told her mother all about our argument except that she'll have twisted it round to make me out as some sort of demented lunatic who got locked up in a house for mad teenagers. She's not really nasty, Fran, but I really hacked her off the last time we met.

Mrs Benson was always a bit funny about my little problem.

She allowed me to take my own shining plates and cutlery to her house and used to say that it was OK to be a 'bit different'.

Whenever she said this she refused to look me in the eye.

'Never mind,' I squeak. 'Market research. I'll call back later.'

I throw the receiver down and wipe my sweaty palms on a brand new tissue from the box by the bed.

This is ridiculous. If I can't even speak to Fran's mother what will I be like when I finally speak to Fran?

Caro's up by midday and ferreting about in the fridge.

'Don't you ever go shopping?' is her charming way of greeting me.

I pull my purse out from my jeans and hand Caro a note.

'Here,' I say. 'Go and get fish and chips for all of us. And don't let them wrap mine in newspaper. Can't eat anything that's been touched by ink.'

Caro scowls and rolls her eyes but she snatches the money. She bangs out of the back door, her iPod blaring as usual, and stomps off down the gravel at the side of the house.

'Yes, very mature!' I say.

I sit down at the kitchen table.

It's very quiet.

No idea when Dad will be back but I really hope he manages to avoid the pub on the way home.

I've got breakfast dishes to wash up and nothing else to do except to see who emailed me that new message on *mysortaspace.com* but just thinking about it and the way that I've

ignored the first email from Alessandro is making me feel kind of sick and guilty and like doing a hundred jumps on the stairs so I try to get that thought out of my mind.

Maybe I could do some – gulp – school-work?

I do thirty-one jumps on the bottom stairs, thirty-one on the top, grab my school bag and come down again doing the same number of jumps on the way back.

I spread out all my nice new exercise books on the disinfected table.

I'm just opening up a thick geography reference book with a sigh of relief when the phone cuts into my thoughts with a shrill ring.

I'm expecting it to be Heather, so I answer the phone in a silly voice.

'House of Homework,' I say. 'Zelah Green speaking from the Rainforests of Brazil.'

There's a short silence and a tiny intake of breath.

I catch my own.

I recognise that breath.

It's Fran.

I'd like to sit down but I'm in the hall and there's no chair so I sit on the floor and lean my back against the wall for support, hoping that there's nothing horrible which will stick to the back of my T-shirt.

Caro has this vile habit of picking her nose or her nails and sticking the gross end result on any passing blank surface.

My breath's coming out in big gulping bursts and my heart is hammering and missing beats and flopping about in a stupid way.

'My mum said that some strange girl rang up pretending to be market research,' says Fran. 'So I thought it must be you.'

Great.

So I'm now known as 'the strange girl' in the Benson household.

'Yeah, it was me actually,' I say. 'Nothing urgent or anything. You didn't really need to call back.'

There's another tense silence.

'OK then,' says Fran. 'Nice talking to you. Bye.'

She's about to hang up when I picture the email lying in wait for me on Heather's computer and shout 'NO! Don't hang up!' in a really uncool kind of way.

Fran stays on the line. I can sense her amusement. She must be loving this. Me about to ask her a favour. Even though it was her who let me down and took away her friendship just when I needed it the most.

I decide to adopt a less desperate tone.

'Right, I'll get to the point,' I say. 'I kind of

got involved in this website thingy. *Mysortaspace. com*. You might have heard of it?'

There's a small splutter of amusement from Fran.

'Yeah,' she says. 'I've heard of it. It's full of people who haven't got any mates.'

I see red, which is really annoying as red stresses me out big-style.

'Fran,' I say. 'I didn't ring you so that you could bitch about me. I rang because I, er,' – here I clear my throat and count to five – 'I kind of need your help. Girl stuff. Because you're good at it,' I add, hoping that a bit of flattery might work wonders.

I wait for the response. I'm pretty sure it's going to be rude and sarcastic.

While I wait I twist around to check there's nothing stuck on my back.

Fran puts her hand over the receiver at the other end. I hear a muffled conversation with

her mother who is making indignant protests in the background interspersed with clanking and kettle-boiling noises.

'In your own time, Fran,' I mutter, but I make sure she can't hear me.

Out of the corner of my eye I see Dad's car pull up outside and Dad getting his briefcase out of the back seat.

My heart starts to hammer all over again. He's got to get this job! He's just got to. For all our sakes . . .

'I said, what sort of girl stuff?' Fran is saying.

I snap back to the present moment.

'You know – just STUFF,' I say. 'Thing is, I don't really know yet. I've kind of heard from this boy. But it's complicated. And I can't talk to Dad because he's got a job interview and he's rubbish at talking about that kind of thing anyway.'

There's another little giggle of amusement.

'Your dad?' says Fran. 'He's actually got a job interview?'

Fran was around when Dad began his horrible descent into a booze-addicted lovesick unemployed nightmare.

'Yes,' I snap. 'Look – either you'll come round here or you won't. Which is it going to be?'

My change of mood must have hit home. Fran's next comment is delivered in a meek sort of whisper.

'OK, I'll come round,' she says. 'This afternoon?'

We agree a time and then Dad's walking in to give me a big virtual hug and Caro's coming in with the fish and chips and just to make me feel even more rubbish, everything gets back to its nightmare crazy chaotic self.

*

Caro's managed to get all the wrong stuff from the fish and chip shop so Dad ends up with a battered sausage when he wanted cod and I end up with plaice even though I prefer haddock and Caro inspects her steak and kidney pie with a puzzled expression, says, 'Oh well,' and eats it as if it's the last piece of food on earth and she's a starving explorer, the sole survivor of a nuclear bomb left combing the earth for unexpected bits of hot junk food.

Dad hasn't said much about his interview.

'Went OK, I think,' is his only comment.

After lunch he goes upstairs, changes out of the smart suit and gets back into his red shirt, old brown trousers and gardening shoes.

He wanders off down the garden with a happy look on his face.

I sigh. Somehow it's hard to imagine Dad back in control of a classroom being enthusiastic

about Shakespeare and Chaucer again.

I'm just wondering whether there are any good vegetable scenes in Shakespeare when Caro says she's got a piece of artwork to do upstairs and it's true that she's really good at art and it helps her cope with her self-harming business so I let her off the washing-up and do it myself as usual but I'm a bit nervous that she might be using the art as an excuse for doing something else, something that involves blood (major *Dirt Alert and Germ Alert*).

I'm all nervous and distracted and have to wash one plate three times because I fail to notice there's a big lump of gluey fish stuck to the bottom.

I keep one eye on the clock as I scrub and scour in my yellow rubber gloves.

Three hours.

Three hours until Fran.

Chapter Nine

At half three Caro's still upstairs and Dad is still down the bottom of the garden. I can see big clods of earth flying up into the air and smoke coming out of his incinerator.

I think about Caro — about how I had this stupid idea that she and I would become great friends after Forest Hill House and that we'd hang out and go to gigs and meet lots of cool and exciting new people, but all that's happened is that she's pissed me off and made the house full of even more *Dirt Alert* and *Germ Alert* than it was before.

And that's saying something.

I'm missing Sol too.

It's getting a bit lonely on Planet Zelah at the moment.

I could do with a friend or two. Or even just one.

I'm in the lounge trying not to look out of the window for Fran but failing.

Every time a blue car goes past my heart thuds and leaps and then when it fails to slow down I get a little mixed pang of relief and disappointment.

'Get a grip!' I say to myself. 'She might be horrid again. This could be a major disaster.'

In some ways today has already been a bit of a disaster. I've quadrupled most of my rituals and even now I'm prodding bits of dirt out from underneath my fingernails with shudders of repulsion.

Will I ever be free of my OCD?

Stella, the therapist in the lovely clean white

coat at the day centre where I go once a fortnight for treatment, thinks that I will be.

I'm not so sure.

'Rome wasn't built in a day,' she says when I complain that it's taking too long to get better.

It's a stupid saying, anyway. Rome was built in about a million years and I can't wait that long to get a cure.

When I say that to Stella she just laughs and flashes her small white teeth.

Stella is the cleanest person on the planet.

I love her.

There's a roar and a screech and Mrs Benson's high blue estate car skids to a halt just past our house.

Great. She's already forgotten where I live. Well, I suppose it has been a while since she dropped Fran off here.

To my surprise Mrs Benson gets out of the

driving seat in her padded green jacket and Wellington boots (useful when you live in Acton) and locks the car door. Followed by Fran, she troops down our front path and raps hard on the door.

I go to let them in with a tight feeling in my chest.

Before I can open my mouth Mrs Benson has pushed past me and is standing in our gloomy hall.

Fran follows her with a small, tight smile.

'Right. Hello, Zelah,' says Mrs Benson in her clipped, professional tone. 'I've brought Fran, seeing as she says it's so important. But if you don't mind, I'd like to hear exactly what it is you are planning to do with her.'

Put like that it sounds as if I'm planning to chop Fran into little bits and boil her up in a cauldron.

That's more something that Caro would do.

86

I swallow hard and invite them into the kitchen.

'Would you like some tea?' I say, trying to remember my manners.

'No, thank you,' says Mrs Benson. Somehow she makes it sound as if I've just offered her a head-slap with a wet cod.

She gestures at the empty chair for me to sit down.

'How long since you left the institution?' she says.

I give her a blank stare.

'Oh,' I say, as the penny drops. 'You mean Forest Hill? It wasn't exactly an institution . . .'

'Yes, well, whatever it was, it was obvious to us that you needed a lot of treatment for your problems,' says Mrs Benson.

I can hardly believe what I'm hearing.

Is this the same woman who smiled at me and let me stay the night and said she was glad

that Fran had such a lovely best friend?

I sit up, very straight.

Fran is flushing scarlet at her mother's words.

'It needed to be said, darling,' says Mrs Benson, ignoring her daughter's squirming embarrassment. 'I'm only looking out for your safety.'

Safety?

What on earth has Fran been telling her mother? That I've morphed into a crazed axe-murderer? (Unlikely, given my well-known hatred of blood and bits of dirty wood.)

There's a sheen of sweat on Fran's smooth tanned face and her dark eyes look scared and helpless.

'Mum,' she says, 'why don't you pick me up in a couple of hours? I'll be fine. Honestly.'

With a show of great reluctance Mrs Benson glares at me, stares down the garden at

the messy vision once known as my father and looks around the kitchen with distaste.

I suppose it could have been worse.

She could have met the other member of our crazy household at the moment.

Thank goodness she didn't have to . . .

'Hi,' says Caro, strolling into the kitchen with a huge piece of cardboard under one arm. She casts a mocking eye over Mrs Benson's Barbour jacket and country boots.

'Jeez,' she splutters. 'Didn't realise you had to get around Acton by *horse*.'

Mrs Benson is rendered speechless with horror, as so often happens when people meet Caro for the first, or even the tenth, time.

She gets up.

'I'll come back at half past five, not a moment later,' she says to Fran as she stalks out of the kitchen. 'It's pony club tonight, remember?'

Caro sniggers.

Mrs Benson leaves a pungent whiff of wet dog and wax jacket behind her. Yuk.

I open the window and cough out of it a few times in order to aerate my lungs.

I notice that Fran has pulled her bag a bit closer and is eyeing Caro with a nervous expression. Well, Caro *is* wearing a Marilyn Manson T-shirt and black combats with silver safety pins all up the sides, matching the one hanging through her eyebrow.

'All right,' says Caro. 'Don't tell me. Let me guess. Fran, right?'

Fran wriggles on her chair and nods.

'How did you know?' she says.

Caro laughs. It is not a friendly sound.

'OCD here told me all about you,' she says.

'It wasn't all my fault,' Fran is saying to Caro. 'Zelah was getting a bit much to handle with her rituals.'

Caro raises one pierced eyebrow, sits down

opposite Fran and gives her a long, hard stare.

'That so?' she says.

Uh-oh. I recognise the signs of a major Caro temper-fest about to strike.

'It's OK,' I say. 'Let's talk about something else. Anyone like some cake?' There's none of my lemon cake left but I'm desperate to avert the impending hurricane.

'Sod the sodding cake,' says Caro, turning to Fran. 'Let me tell you something, little girl.'

Fran makes an indignant little-girl squeal of protest. She's only one year younger than Caro but she does look a lot more innocent when you compare her pink dress, neat brown plaits and shoes with little flowers to Caro's big black baggy outfit.

'Anybody who upsets my best mate OCD here,' and Caro tilts her blonde head towards me with a sharp gesture, 'has me to reckon with. OK?'

Fran turns pale and then flushes pink.

This is a total nightmare. And since when did Caro become my best friend? 'That's enough,' I say. The iron in my voice takes us all by surprise. 'Leave Fran alone. She's come to help me with something.'

'Oh, have I?' mutters Fran. 'That's news to me. I haven't actually agreed to do anything yet.'

She looks at my gritted teeth and hands-on-hips posture and shuts up.

'I'll give you my blue sparkly earrings,' I say. Fran always used to stare at them with longing when she thought I wasn't looking.

'Done,' says Fran.

'Yeah, excuse me interrupting your business transactions but I'll have that cake now,' says Caro. She manages to make it sound as if she's doing me a massive favour by suggesting this.

Oh great. I'm going to have to demonstrate some more OCD weirdness now.

I scrabble around the bottom of the cake tin with my rubber gloves to avoid contamination by old sponge and find an ancient Battenberg. I cut two slices for Fran and Caro (I don't do out-of-date cake – major *Germ Alert*) and we sit in silence.

The girls make a great play of separating the pink and yellow squares and peeling off long sticky strips of marzipan. It's like watching a children's television presenter trying to make something, except without the happy smiles and silly music.

I check my watch. We've already wasted loads of time arguing so I take Fran upstairs and leave Caro smoking and casting the evil eye at Fran's neat departing bottom in its flowery dress.

Fran struts out of the kitchen with her nose stuck in the air.

*

Fran waits for me while I do my jumps on the stairs.

I can see her biting her tongue and trying to be patient.

It's all a bit awkward.

And sad.

We used to chat away without pausing for breath in the back of the biology lesson, collecting detentions like Smarties. When we weren't chatting we were texting and when we weren't texting we were either on the phone every evening catching up on gossip or emailing each other in the dead of night.

How can five years of chatting turn into this awkward moment of tension on the staircase?

But that's what's happened.

She follows me into my bedroom, glancing around at the gleaming white walls and bleached-white pillowcases, sniffing the sterilised air.

'Still got the OCD, then?' is all she says, but it's enough.

I flush and look down at my silver flip-flops.

'Never mind that,' I say. 'I need your advice please. I've got this email from a boy and I don't know whether to reply to it or not.'

Fran gives me a look of disbelief.

'You've got me here just to read one email from one boy?' she says. 'Zelah. I can't believe you rang me up just because of that.'

I flush again and chew my lip.

'OK,' I say. 'I maybe could have read the email on my own. But I don't know how I'm going to react after reading it, do I?'

Fran raises a pretty arched eyebrow at me until I sink down on to the edge of the bed.

'Fine,' I say. 'So I'm having a lonely holiday. I admit it. But I do really need your help with the email from this boy.'

Fran tosses her shiny plaits back and takes off her smart denim jacket, hanging it over the back of a chair and sitting down at my desk. She clicks open a designer glasses-case and slides a pair of expensive-looking pink frames up her nose.

'Fine, let me see it,' she says.

I flip open Heather's laptop and click on to the first email from Alessandro. Fran reads it in silence and then screws her mouth up to one side.

'Well,' she says. 'The heavy metal bit is gross. Maybe he should hook up with your friend downstairs instead,' and she tips her head in a dismissive way towards the open door.

'But he doesn't sound like a teen-killer, if that's what you're worried about.'

I wonder if Fran's forgotten to read the very last bit of the email so I point at the screen (not actually touching it, of course,

because smudges are *Dirt Alert* and then I'd have to go and get a clean white cloth to wipe it off).

'Yeah, so?' says Fran in a voice quite at odds with her neat pink girly appearance. 'Loads of people have parents in prison. Welcome to the twenty-first century, Zelah. I mean – there's like nothing remarkable about that, is there? You were locked up in Forest Hill with all those weirdos. You should know about strange people by now.'

I take a deep calming breath. I know full well that Fran's just approving of jailbait fathers because it's the opposite of what I'm expecting her to do.

Difficult. She's a difficult ex-best friend.

There's still that new email from Alessandro so I click on it with my arm trembling.

It only asks whether I got his first email.

'So you think I should write back?' I say.

'S'pose I have been quite rude ignoring his mails.'

Fran stands up to offer me the chair and then she looks over my shoulder and in a grudging, impatient sort of way, helps me to write a reply. This is what we come up with:

Dear Alessandro.

Thanks for your two emails. Yes my name really IS Zelah. I don't think there's anything weird about it but then again I'm used to it. I live with my demented father in West London and at the moment I've got a friend called Caro staying with me. She's into Marilyn Manson in a big way and for some unknown reason my father thinks she's the best thing since stale sliced white loaf. I haven't got many hobbies 'cos I haven't got time to do anything much other than try to get my father to job interviews and clean the house from top to bottom. But that's another story. And by the way, sorry to hear that your father is in jail. Bummer. Anyway, write again soon. Zelah.

I don't put 'love' or anything crazy like that. Don't want to give out false signals.

Fran spellchecks the email and then I press the send button and my message to Alessandro whizzes off into cyberspace and my legs have gone all shaky and bloodless so I sit down hard on the end of my nice clean duvet and Fran goes off downstairs to make us some tea with sugar in.

'I only use the white cup with the red flowers on!' I shout downstairs after her.

I know it's a bit pathetic, but that's my own special cup.

Nobody else dares to drink from the Cup of Zelah.

Fran spends the rest of the afternoon trying on all my earrings and experimenting with my make-up while she tells me how fantastic her life is and how shit mine must be.

At five thirty she stands up, snaps her rosebud-framed glasses back into their silver designer case and pulls on her smart Gap denim jacket.

I pass her the blue sparkly earrings in total silence and she tucks them into her beaded purse.

Outside Mrs Benson is making a great play of revving her monstrous engine and ruining the environment while looking at her wrist-watch, tapping her fingernails on the side of the car and mouthing the word 'pony'.

'OK then,' says Fran. 'Let me know if he writes back or if he wants to meet you 'cos you like *so* need serious wardrobe advice.'

'Thank you,' I say, in the same formal voice she's just used.

We shuffle down the dark poky hallway trying not to touch one another and I accompany her down the front path.

Of course I can't touch anybody anyway, because of my problem. But Fran doesn't have that problem.

She must hate me.

'OK then, bye,' she says, running towards her mother's car with ill-disguised relief. Running away from the crazy household where the depressed father, the devil-worshipper and the axe-murdering psycho with the rituals live in disharmony.

'Bye,' I say in a small, sad voice.

Then I walk back towards home. Ha. That's a joke.

My home is full of stress.

I've forgotten how to do fun teenaged things.

This is one of the worst summers. Ever.

Chapter Ten

Three days later and no reply from Alessandro.

I'm sure I've put him off with my stupid email and the weird thing is that even though I didn't really want to write to him I'm kind of annoyed that he hasn't written back.

But there's a new email waiting for me on Heather's laptop this morning.

It's from somebody called 'Marky' and just his name is enough to make me feel really edgy and unsettled.

I don't like names with extra letters on the end. They're not neat and as you might have

guessed by now, I like things to be neat and tidy.

The email says that he's sixteen, tall, fair-haired, loves sailing and playing tennis and in his spare time he invents computer games.

I want to be a millionaire by the time I'm twenty, he puts at the very end of the message. *And I'm the youngest ever contestant to go on* Dragon's Den.

'Huh,' I snort as I read this bit. I'm not impressed by money. Good job really as Dad never has any and I have to buy most of my clothes off eBay.

Then I notice that Marky has added a photograph to his profile so I click on it in a not-really-bothered kind of way and this really handsome guy pops up grinning at me from a tanned face and with kind blue eyes and I think: *Oh well, what the heck. Might as well reply,* and before I know it I've written him a three-page epic all about my life and

pressed the 'send' button before becoming a shaking wreck.

I've scrubbed my face about fifty times this morning, which is twenty times more than usual.

My skin is stinging and smarting so much that I take one of Dad's painkillers to try and calm it down.

I'm back in my bedroom reading a website called 'Addicted to Disastrous Dating and how to get over it' when Dad comes bounding upstairs and bursts in.

'Zelah, emergency!' he pants before running straight out again.

I slam the lid of the laptop shut and leap up, alarmed.

What now? Has Caro set fire to the house or invited Marilyn Manson around for a spot of group devil-worship?

I rush downstairs into the kitchen where Dad is pacing back and forth with a piece of paper in his hand.

There's no sign of Caro.

'What's happened? Where's Caro?' I say.

Dad gives me a puzzled look.

'In bed. Where else?' he says. 'It's only eleven o'clock.'

'Dad,' I say. 'Just tell me what this emergency is.'

Dad passes me the letter with a shaking hand.

I take it by the tips of my fingernails and place it on the table.

'Dear Mr Green,' it says. 'We are delighted to offer you the position of English Teacher at Smithfield High School, Acton W3. Please report to the School Secretary's office on Monday 12 August when you will be expected to complete a two-week induction course

before the commencement of Autumn Term.

Yours sincerely, Ms S. Smart, School Secretary.'

Lots of things whizz through my bemused brain.

The first is: how exactly is this an emergency?

The second thought eclipses this one. Dad has got a job! He's actually gone and got a job!

The third thought is that if Dad has a job, I'm going to be spending a lot of time on my own.

And the fourth thought is: when will Caro be going back to her foster parents? Because she's left school already and if Dad is out all day, Caro will be living in our house on her own and I will have to come home from school Every Single Day and find her there, like some gross evil young stepmother or something . . .

'Well?' Dad is saying. 'Can't you say

anything? Are you pleased for me, Princess?'

I skip over and give Dad a virtual hug, without arms or anything.

'Yay!' I say. 'You got a job! That's fantastic.'

Then I run back upstairs and check my emails for about the billionth time.

Nothing.

I have to grab the disinfectant and perform a major clean of the black laptop keyboard even though it doesn't really need one.

My little problem appears to be getting worse, what with Caro's grumpy behaviour and the uncertainty of emailing strange boys on the computer.

Here I go, heading off to jump on the stairs.

Again.

I get a tiny bit of homework done on Saturday morning in between clearing up breakfast and going shopping so that we have food. I write

about ten words of an essay on 'The Wife of Bath' by Chaucer. Just the title of the book is enough to cheer me up. I have a great relationship with baths.

Not keen on the brown scum-line left around the sides afterwards though. *Dirt Alert.*

Spurred on by the bath connection I take one straight after doing my schoolwork.

I lie in a mass of fragrant lime bubbles and enjoy some good 'phoo, phoo,' breaths with my hand on my soapy chest, trying to have a nice calming moment.

As if.

Caro's hammering on the bathroom door.

'OCD!' she yells. 'I need to get in. Pronto!'

'Can't it wait?' I yell back. 'I'm having a calm bath. It's part of my therapy. Stella has prescribed it.'

This is a complete lie of course, but it's the only way I can think of getting Caro to

leave me in peace. Despite being a total nightmare about nearly everything, she gets the therapy thing.

She should do – she's had enough of it.

'Oh, OK,' she says. There's a pause when I sense she's still hovering outside the bathroom door and then her bedroom door bangs and the oh-so-familiar growl of Marilyn Manson rises up from the fiery abyss of Hell.

I'm a bit worried that I know all the lyrics off by heart now.

I'm even singing along underneath the bubbles.

By the time I get out of my bath I'm all shrivelled and dried-up but I don't care.

I'm super-ultra clean and hygienic.

'Hooray,' I say to my scrubbed reflection in the mirror.

I treat myself to a new pot of talc, twisting the dial on top and shaking the sweet clean

powder all over my scrubbed bits.

'Marvellous,' I say.

I turn the bathroom door handle and am about to skip to my bedroom and select some lovely clean clothes when something tells me to look down.

There's a big patch of something red on the carpet beneath my feet.

'Oh shit,' I say.

She's started to do it again.

Chapter Eleven

O^{K.}
     This is a major *Dirt Alert* and *Germ Alert* moment.

I am standing on a carpet right next to a big patch of blood and I have bare feet.

Nightmare.

I hop back into the safety of the bathroom.

There are two white flannels sealed into plastic bags. Heather steals them from hotels for me because she knows I like them.

I tie one flannel around each foot and then put the plastic bag over the top so I look like I'm wearing some weird space-age baby

bootees but I'm past caring what I look like by now.

Then I close my eyes and tiptoe around the blood in my strange padded feet, shuddering at each step.

I knock on Caro's door.

'Caro?'

No reply.

'Can I come in, please?' I say. My voice has a schoolteacher prissiness that I hate.

There's still no answer.

Great.

This is just what I need. Blood and maybe even potential death on a Saturday afternoon when I should be doing my homework.

I sigh and push open the door with one fingernail.

Caro's lying on her back on the bed and staring up at the ceiling, hugging her own elbows.

I can hear the drumbeat blaring from her iPod so I step forward and pull one earplug out of her ear.

'Put that back,' says Caro. She sounds faint and weary.

'No,' I say. 'Not until you tell me what you're playing at.'

Caro swivels up into a sitting position and regards my feet.

'OCD, what the hell are you wearing?' she says.

I ignore this.

'Show me your arms,' I say.

For answer, Caro pulls down the long sleeves of her black top and hugs her arms closer. She looks like a daddy-long-legs after it's been half-murdered by a playful cat – all angles and bent bits.

'Caro,' I say. 'For God's sake show me your arms and then I can help you.'

Caro gives a bitter little laugh.

'You, OCD?' she says. 'You're not in a fit state to help anyone. I heard you doing about a million jumps last night.'

'Yeah, and I wonder why that is?' I say. 'Maybe it's because I have the psycho house guest from hell staying in my spare bedroom.'

'She sounds fun!' says Caro. 'Do introduce us when she next visits.'

I stand up in my rustling bootees and make an inelegant waddle for the door.

Just as I get there Caro swings her legs off the bed and says, 'OK, OK. Come back.'

As this is about the nearest Caro ever gets to apologising, I come back in and sit on the bed.

'Here,' she says.

She pulls back her long sleeves and reveals a new section of fresh criss-cross slashes across the soft white underneath of her arm.

'Ooh, giddy,' I say, putting my head between my knees.

I'm terrible with blood.

When I come up again I swear Caro's almost smiling.

'OCD, you freak me out, man,' she says. 'Only you could end up, like, twisting this all around so that now I'm worried about you.'

What?

'Since when have you ever worried about me?' I say. This is a true surprise. Nothing Caro does or says ever shows any scrap of concern for my health.

Unless you count verbal abuse and spitting and snarling as concern.

'You'd be surprised,' says Caro in an enigmatic sort of way.

Then she goes pale green and clammy and I realise I'm going to have to do something about the blood coming out of her arms so I

untie my feet-flannels and wrap them around her wrists with a shudder. Then I lock the door. This would not be a good moment for Dad to come in and request lunch.

I sit on the bed for about an hour until I'm sure the bleeding has stopped.

We don't talk much, but that's because Caro decides to play me the new Marilyn Manson album and I have to pretend to love it.

Just as I'm finally leaving the room with a pounding headache, she says: 'It's not really working out with my foster parents.'

'I thought that your foster mother sounded all right on the phone,' I say. Caro's pale face is making me feel sorry for her, but my hair's dried in damp rat-tails over my face and any moment now Dad will peel off his gardening gloves and head towards the kitchen for a limp cheese sandwich.

Caro gives her sarcastic little laugh again.

'Yeah, she's nice,' she says. 'That's the problem. Next to her I look, like, really really evil.'

I decide not to point out that even next to the devil himself, Caro would still look, like, really really evil.

'So what are you going to do?' I say. I'm shivering now.

'Well, stay here as long as poss and then speak to Social Services, I suppose,' says Caro. 'See if I can get plonked with another couple of idiots who don't understand me.'

It sounds like a lost cause to me but I don't say this. I'm desperate for the loo now and starving hungry as well as freezing cold. And I just don't know what to say.

I give Caro an apologetic smile.

'I hope it works out,' I say. 'I really do. Oh – and I hope you don't mind me asking. But could you dispose of those bloody flannels, please?'

Then I bolt out of the door.

The three of us manage to eat lunch together without having a big argument. I see Dad glance at Caro's arms and he refrains from asking why she is wearing long sleeves in the middle of a heatwave, but she sees the look and gives him some old rubbish about having a sun allergy, which is kind of true. Like all devil-worshippers she prefers to be pale and interesting and encourage that 'just dug up' look rather than aspiring to be brown and wrinkled like the rest of us.

We eat cheese sandwiches in companionable silence and I wash up afterwards while Caro and Dad roll up about sixty cigarettes and talk about old dead rock stars (again).

After lunch I go upstairs and try not to check my email but I do. Still nothing from Alessandro but there's a message from some

boy called Daz who's got a pit bull terrier which means that I have to totally ignore the email as dogs and cats are major *Dirt Alert* and *Germ Alert*. Oh, and there's a short reply from Marky.

I live in Shepherd's Bush, he says. *How about we meet up on Saturday? Bring a mate of course.*

Too right I'll take a mate. I'm hardly going to take time out of my busy schedule to meet some unknown nutter all on my own and in any case it's a policy of *mysortaspace.com* that you have to take somebody with you for security.

I wonder if Fran will agree to come with me?

I whizz off a quick reply suggesting that we meet outside the Central Line tube station and then I continue my essay on 'The Wife of Bath' and I feel, if not exactly cheerful, then kind of resigned to the next few days.

So – Dad's going to be at the new school all week and that means I've got to deal with Caro on my own and make sure that if Fran comes on Saturday, she and Caro don't kill each other and that Caro stops cutting her arms and finds something positive to focus on.

This has all kind of become my life now.

My jumps have gone up to fifty on the top step and fifty on the bottom step and my face-scrubs are creeping up again too. I did fifty scrubs on each cheek this morning and brushed my hair an extra twenty-two times.

'Just another day in the crap life of Zelah Green,' I say.

Chapter Twelve

Monday comes and Dad's up at the crack of dawn polishing his best work shoes and squirting himself with some choke-inducing aftershave.

He stirs his muesli around the bowl about a million times and keeps clearing his throat and checking the clock.

'D'you know, Princess, I think I'm a bit nervous?' he says as he ties the laces on his shoes to the exact same length.

'I'd never have guessed, Dad,' I say, but my sarcasm is wasted on him. He doesn't 'do' sarcasm very often. Dad's specialities are being

pathetic, wounded, hopeless and depressed rather than sarcastic.

He throws his cereal bowl into the sink with a clatter and straightens his tie.

'How do I look?' he says.

I appraise my smart, teacher Dad from top to bottom.

'Not bad,' I say. 'Don't forget to smile.'

Dad flashes a fake stiff grin.

'Heather would be proud of you,' I say. 'And Mum would too.'

Dad winks at me for that and pretends to ruffle my hair.

Hooray. A glimmer of the old Dad has flashed through the building.

I wave him off from the front doorstep just like Mum used to do. Spooky.

Then I clear up all the breakfast things and check my email.

There's a confirmation from Marky saying

that he'll be waiting for me on Saturday outside the tube station in Shepherd's Bush.

And – there's one from Alessandro!

I've still got Fran on speeddial on my mobile.

She says she'll be round in half an hour.

To my amazement mixed with more than a smidgen of horror, Caro gets up early and comes down for breakfast.

'Thought I'd see what this morning thing looks like,' she says, tipping cornflakes into a bowl and pouring apple juice all over them.

I'm about to protest at such shocking abuse of innocent corn cereal but then I think better of it. Caro does look a bit pale and unhappy this morning. Her arms are healing up, or so she says when I ask her.

Anyway, I know full well why she's dragged herself out of her pit at this ungodly hour.

She must have overheard me talking on my mobile.

She wants to keep an eye on Fran.

Fran's as punctual as ever.

'Hi,' she says. There's even a small smile. It's a pathetic cousin of the big grin she would have given me once upon a time, but it's a start.

She's holding out a warm paper bag towards me.

'Croissants,' she says. 'And there are some clean tissues in there.'

I'm touched.

'Thanks,' I say. 'Come in. We're in the kitchen.'

Fran's face clouds over a bit at the 'we' part of my sentence.

She follows me slowly into the kitchen where Caro is rolling a cigarette.

'Oh, erm, hello again,' says Fran in her posh-girl party voice.

'Hmm,' says Caro.

Well – it's more of a piggish grunt, really.

The two of them sit there in silence while I make a pot of tea and get plates for the food.

Caro brightens up a bit when she sees croissants. Fran has brought four, so that she and I can have two each, but Caro delves into the bag and comes up triumphant with the biggest one.

'Cheers, Fanny,' she says, biting off the corner with her small sharp teeth.

'Fran,' says Fran. 'My name is Fran.'

'Oops,' says Caro. She eyes up Fran's pink pinafore dress and white plimsolls.

'You do look a bit like a Fanny though, if you don't mind me saying so.'

Fran is bristly and blinking with indignation like a hedgehog pulled out of the ground

before the end of hibernation.

'And you look a bit like a . . .' she starts, but I plonk the teapot down on the table just in time.

'Tea?' I say, in a loud bright voice.

Fran and Caro are eyeing one another up like a pair of tomcats.

Any moment now there's going to be hissing and fur flying. Not to mention huge gaping wounds. Major *Germ Alert*, obviously. There are many reasons I don't like cats.

'Yes please, one sugar,' says Fran. She takes the cup and sips with her little finger pointing out in a delicate fashion.

Caro sniggers and blows a huge smoke ring up into the air.

'Ooh, tea party! How lovely,' she says, mimicking Fran's voice. 'And will you be having cucumber sandwiches?'

I grip the underside of my chair, even

though I know it's not as clean as I'd like.

Fran, you see, is very sweet and posh and all that, but if you wind her up, as well I know, she can go bonkers with rage.

Fran must be trying hard to stay polite because she gives me a tiny smile.

'How long do you think I'll be here today, Zelah?' she says.

Ah-ha! So that's how she's going to play it. Ignore Caro. Pretend she doesn't exist.

Big, big mistakerola.

If there's one thing that Caro can't bear, it's being ignored.

She might as well have 'I must be the centre of attention at all times,' tattooed on her forehead.

'Hey,' says Caro, tipping the kitchen table up towards Fran so that her plate of croissant starts to slither towards her. 'I'm talking to you. Didn't you hear me, little girl?'

Fran lifts her nose slightly and sniffs.

'Right, Zelah, I'll eat this and then I'll get to work,' she says, ignoring Caro again.

I'm holding my breath now. This is terrible. I can't eat my croissant because my mouth has dried to cobwebs.

Fran is about to pick up her breakfast and take a dainty bite, but Caro has other ideas.

The croissant, still on its plate, slides off the table and into Fran's lap as Caro lifts her side up higher and higher.

Then with an enormous slam she drops it back on the floor again and pushes back her chair.

'You're a complete arsehole!' she screams before storming out of the room and banging the door.

A selection of coloured fridge magnets falls on to the floor.

Fran picks up the plate and the greasy flakes

of jam and pastry from her pink dress and reassembles them on the table.

'How do you put up with that?' she says, eating the less ruined of two croissants.

I admire the way she's not crying or making a fuss.

I would be.

'Dunno, really,' I say. I've got mixed feelings at the moment. A big part of me wants to slap Caro for being so rude to my friend. Or ex-friend, I suppose.

Another part of me knows that Caro is lonely and insecure and unhappy and thinks that Fran is going to take me away and leave Caro deserted on an island of self-harm with only the dire songs of Marilyn Manson and a limp pouch of tobacco worms for company.

'Caro isn't as horrid as she comes across,' I say in the end.

Fran raises her eyebrows but says nothing.

'Come on,' she says. 'We've got work to do.'

The clash between Fran and Caro has made me all tense and unsettled.

When Fran goes to the loo I make an excuse and creep upstairs to do some rituals.

I do fifty jumps on the carpet in my bedroom and then measure all the gaps between my clothes in the wardrobe with a ruler, just to make sure that they are exactly four centimetres apart.

Fran comes in and gives me a look of impatience but I can't stop.

'Sorry,' I say. 'Give me ten minutes.'

I tidy my bedroom up and make all the spines of my books stand up straight and tall in the bookcase.

Then I stick some washing in the machine downstairs and clean the kitchen table.

Only when I've done all that can I face going back up to my bedroom.

And that turns out to be a hideous mistake.

First thing is that Caro has followed Fran up there and is sitting on my bed with her dirty boots all over the white duvet.

Fran is sitting at my desk with her back towards Caro. It's a back as hard and rigid as a plank of wood so I can see that she's not enjoying Caro's company.

'Caro,' I say. 'Haven't you anything else to do? Painting? Smoking? Abusing strangers on the street?'

I gesture towards Fran and make some encouraging faces but Caro fails to pick up on my hint. On purpose.

'OCD, are you trying to get rid of me?' she says. 'That hurts, man.'

I sigh loudly.

'It's kind of private,' I say. 'I'll be down in half an hour. Promise.'

'Ooh,' says Caro, her face lighting up with malice. 'I bet it's BOY stuff. Hey, Fanny! Got a boyfriend? I heard you were a bit of a tease.'

'I haven't got time for a boyfriend,' says Fran in a low, neutral voice meant to discourage any further conversation.

'Haven't got a boyfriend?' Caro says, her eyes glinting at having found a chink in Fran's armour.

'Why not? Do you bat for the other side? Or are you like OCD here? Boys are just a germ-carrying waste of space. Unless they happen to be called Sol.'

I make to whack Caro over the head.

'Hey! No need for that!'

I don't want Caro spilling the details of my disastrous love life to my ex-best friend.

Fran's back goes even stiffer and she pretends

to be reading the screen on Heather's laptop even though it hasn't fired up into life yet.

'Ahh, diddums,' says Caro, on a roll now. 'Poor little Fanny hasn't got a boyfriend! Maybe they don't like her perfect pink clothes and her sweet little plaits. Maybe they'd prefer a *real* woman like me. Or maybe she's frigid! That's it! Frigid Fanny!'

Caro lies right back on my bed with a satisfied smirk on her skinny features.

She drums a pen on the edge of my bookshelf and hums an irritating tune to herself.

Fran is turning puce.

'Why don't you go back downstairs and smoke yourself to death?' she says, turning round and directing the full force of her Franglare upon Caro.

Caro lights up like a crazed Christmas tree.

She gets another pen and starts drumming two at the same time, still singing an

annoying little riff over and over.

All I can see is a big grassy clump of vile mud dangling off the sole of Caro's boot.

Any moment now that clump is going to fall off and attach itself to my bed.

MAJOR DIRT ALERT.

Fran gets up from her chair and starts to advance on Caro.

'Right,' she says. 'That's it. Get out of Zelah's bedroom. Now.'

Caro does a pretend tremble but I notice that her smile has faded just a bit.

'I'm not joking,' says Fran.

I half expect to see actual steam coming out of her ears so I duck.

Fran leans over the bed and Caro's pretending to squeal in fright but is really enjoying herself in that warped way of hers and I've just about had enough of this now.

'Right,' I say. 'Caro. Downstairs. NOW.

And please take that duvet cover with you. I want it boil-washed at ninety degrees and then rinsed in fabric softener. Then I want it hung on the washing line, attached only with the blue plastic pegs from the packet NOT the dirty wooden ones. Goddit?'

Wow. I sound like one of my teachers.

Caro swings her legs off the bed, still with the insolent grin on her face. She picks up the whole duvet despite my desperate cries and drags it off into the hallway, muttering and swearing as she goes.

The smell of stale tobacco hangs in the air.

I fling open my sparkling latticed windows and let a cool breeze stream in.

Fran takes her coat off and lets out a sigh of relief.

'How do you put up with her?' she says. 'And WHY do you put up with her?'

I sigh too.

'It's complicated,' I say. 'She kind of helped me at Forest Hill. And Dad thinks she's a reborn angel.'

Fran looks very doubtful at this but manages not to say anything nasty.

I go downstairs and get us a can of coke each from the fridge and then I show her the emails and photo from Marky.

'Wow, Zelah,' she says. 'He's got a stupid name but he's hot! If you don't like him, can I have him?'

She's not joking either. And the annoying thing is that when I turn up with Fran in tow this Marky will probably take one look at her beautiful long brown hair and freckled face and fall head over heels in love with her and that will be me out of the frame forever.

Then I open the latest email from Alessandro. This is what it says:

Dear Zelah,

Sorry, I hope I didn't upset you by mentioning your weird name. I guess I kind of like it that's all. Cheers for mentioning my dad. He's doing OK in the nick now. He's got this cellmate called Chris who weighs about ninety stone and has fifteen snakes tattooed on his left arm. So nobody bothers them much. Which is good 'cos my dad's quite a small bloke. What do you do at the weekends? I'm going on hols for a week but maybe we could meet up some time after that? Your profile says that you live in West London. I live over East London but I could get a tube. I understand if you want to bring somebody with. I mean, I could be anybody. But I'm not. I'm just me. Alessandro. x.

'He put a kiss! He put a kiss!' squeals Fran in this demented fashion.

'Er, it's only one,' I say, but inside I feel all pleased and hot.

137

I've stopped Fran and Caro from killing each other and Alessandro has put a kiss on his email.

Maybe things are finally looking up.

Chapter Thirteen

Fran's agreed to come with me to meet Marky on Saturday morning. I reckon she just wants to flirt with him and lure him away, but seeing as how I'm not exactly swamped with friends at the moment it's Fran or nothing.

Dad would go mental if he found out I was going off to meet a strange boy so I've sworn Fran to secrecy and also made her promise upon pain of violent death that she won't tell Caro.

Dad comes home at half four when Fran has

left with promises to return on Saturday morning with some story worked out about what she and I are supposed to be doing all that day.

Caro is upstairs downloading new goth misery music from Heather's computer on to her iPod.

I'm sitting at the kitchen table performing a ritual on the last of the custard creams by dissecting it into little squares of equal sizes and arranging the pieces around the edge of the plate with four centimetres in between them.

'Oh dear,' says Dad when he sees this. 'Bad day, Princess?'

He throws his briefcase into the corner and pulls out a chair.

His eyes are a bit red and his cheeks are flushed and there is a faint whiff of something. Petrol? Aftershave?

Oh no, it's stale beer.

'Dad,' I begin, suddenly feeling as if I have the weight of the entire world on my shoulders. 'Dad, please tell me you didn't go in the pub on the way home from school?'

Dad holds his hands up in a surrender position. His tie is hanging loose around his neck in a most un-teacherly fashion.

'OK, I did go for one quick drink,' he says. 'But only because I was celebrating my first day in a proper job again. The induction is going really well.'

I perk up a bit at that. He does look cheerful, in a flushed kind of way.

'What were the other teachers like?' I say.

Dad gets up and clicks on the kettle.

'Nice,' he says. 'Yep. They were really nice. I think I'm going to like it there.'

Well, at least something good has come out of this confusing day. My father is

finally getting himself sorted.

I dissect the custard cream into even smaller bits.

Then I go upstairs to scrub my face.

Chapter Fourteen

My rituals go from bad to worse.

When I was at Forest Hill I kind of got over my fear of touching toilets and sinks. But now it all seems to be going backwards again.

I've just been to see Stella at the clinic for my treatment session.

It's fair to say that she wasn't very happy with my progress.

Stella looked as hygienic as ever in her white coat and shoes.

But she didn't smile as much as usual. Her face kept creasing into a frown as she listened

to me talk about what was going on at home.

'So you're pretty much trying to take control of everything,' she said. It's not really a question, more just a summing-up of my hideous life.

She chewed her lip for a moment and I got all worried that she was considering contacting Social Services and reporting Dad for going to the pub on the way home from teaching and not helping me with the cleaning.

And if she got them involved they might take me away from home and place me with foster parents. Like Caro. Look what's happened to her.

'It's only temporary,' I said, trying to smile. 'Heather's back in a couple of weeks and then I'll be able to get on with my normal school life after that.'

'Hmm,' said Stella. 'The thing is, Zelah, that none of the things happening in your house should really be your responsibility

at all. I'm not surprised that your rituals are getting worse.'

After a bit more of her looking doubtful and me pleading that everything at home would soon be normal again (ha!) she let me go home on the condition that I ring her up if it all gets too much.

Like I'm going to do that. I might as well just ring social services direct and volunteer myself as a homeless foster child.

'It's fine. It'll be fine,' I said as I backed out of her office and made a run for the bus.

Saturday dawns all wet and horrid.

Great. I won't even be able to wear my favourite silver flip-flops unless I want to make weird squelching noises all around Shepherd's Bush.

I'm up in the bathroom doing some extra rituals to prepare.

I turn the taps with a tissue wedged between the cold metal and my warm hand.

I put a piece of paper on the toilet seat before I sit on it.

If I forget to wash my hands at any time I have to do each hand an extra thirty times, with the nailbrush and a load of white soap.

The soap has to be a brand new fresh bar and not an old slimy brown one.

All my pocket money (when Dad remembers to give it to me) has been spent on soaps in cellophane wrappers over the last few weeks.

Other kids are going to the cinema or lying in the park eating ice creams or hanging around clothes shops with their friends or going to Disney Land or going up to London by train to see a show.

And me?

I'm sitting on the toilet trying not to touch it with any bits of my skin and I'm worried

about going on a date with a strange boy who could turn out to be some creepy old man for all I know and my ex-best friend probably pities me because I've made such a mess of things and she hates my other sort-of-friend Caro, who hates her, and she regards Dad as a bit of a weirdo and I'm not sure Dad's all that happy in his new job and Sol's somewhere out there in the big wide world and I'm all unsure what to do about Alessandro and . . . and . . .

'OCD!'

Caro is banging on the bathroom door. Not again.

'Please tell me you haven't produced more blood,' I shout. 'If you have then you'll just have to drown in it. I am not coming out until I am ready.'

'Your little friend Fanny is here!' she yells.

Fran's nearly an hour early.

Great.

'Make her some tea,' I yell. 'And be NICE.'

I hear Caro's evil little chuckle and my heart sinks further towards the bottom of the (very clean) toilet bowl.

How on earth do I get into these situations?

I dry off with a nice clean white towel and do fifty jumps on the bathroom mat.

By the time I've finished scrubbing my face, brushing my hair and cleaning my teeth Caro has been up twice to complain.

'Jeez, OCD,' she hisses through the bathroom door. 'Can't your sodding rituals wait? I'm stuck downstairs with Frigid Fanny.'

'Just a minute,' I hiss back.

I need to finish off by cleaning my teeth with my left hand. Don't ask me why. I've already done them with my right, but somehow my brain is telling me that I can't say I've completed my rituals until I've done them with the left hand too.

Another weird moment in the life of Zelah Green.

When I get downstairs I ban Caro from following me upstairs with Fran by bribing her with money.

Then Fran and I tip all the contents of my wardrobe on to the bed and Fran starts rifling through them with a frown on her smooth brown forehead.

'Zelah, you like, *so* need to update your capsule wardrobe,' she says.

I ignore the insult and allow her to hold a long red flippy skirt in front of me and team it up with a white vest top.

'Yeah, that's nice,' she says. 'Kind of girly but casual.'

My heart does somersaults of guilt 'cos Dad bought me that skirt last year and it's my favourite and now I'm lying to

Dad about where I'm going today.

Dad looked a bit suspicious when Fran said that we were going to the cinema and then out for pizza.

'You two girls seem to be getting on very well again,' he said. 'Didn't you have some major bust-up a few weeks back? Didn't I hear you say, Zelah, that you'd rather plunge your hands into an un-flushed toilet than ever clap eyes on Fran again?'

I went puce with embarrassment.

Dad's not great at being tactful.

Fran got her revenge straight away. She looked him right in the eye – she's a fabulous liar – and said, 'Yeah, but I've forgiven Zelah now. After all, she does have a lot to put up with.'

I felt like murdering her when she said this.

Her forgive ME?

It wasn't me who confessed that rituals

made her feel ill.

Or me who said that everyone at school thought I was a weirdo.

But Dad seemed to swallow the lie so I bit my tongue and said nothing.

Fran sits me in front of the mirror and plugs in her portable hair straighteners.

'There,' she says, smoothing my strands of black frizz into something sleeker and less wiry.

I look at her reflection. She's biting her lip with concentration as she coaxes and twists my black locks.

'Fran,' I say. 'Why are you doing this? I mean – you made it really clear at Forest Hill what you thought about my rituals and everything.'

Fran continues her careful straightening of my hair but her eye catches mine for a moment in the mirror.

She finishes what she's doing and unplugs the straighteners.

'Well, actually,' she says, running a brush through my new smooth hair, 'I've kind of – missed you. A bit.'

We both turn the colour of purple grapes and Fran turns round and begins to sort through my flip-flop collection.

'I've missed you too,' I say. I busy myself applying lipgloss with a small sticky brush. 'In fact, I've got a brand new word for you.'

I always used to come up with a 'word of the day' for Fran when we were friends before.

Fran turns round from the wardrobe.

'Yeah?' she says. 'What is it?'

'Renaissance,' I say. 'It means you can do loads of different creative things.'

We exchange cautious smiles.

It's a start.

*

By the time I've finished getting ready it's nearly time to leave for the tube.

I stand in front of the mirror.

'Not bad,' I say. In fact I look pretty good.

I'm wearing a white vest top, the long red skirt, brown boots, and Fran has lent me her cut-off denim jacket to put over the top.

I hook a pair of long red sparkly earrings through my ears and spray a nice new clean can of shine spray all over my sleek hair.

'You look really nice, Zelah,' says Fran in a soft voice.

I smile, although I'm a bit worried about my red cheeks.

Maybe scrubbing my face wasn't such a good idea. Like I have any control over it.

'Thanks,' I say.

We shout goodbye to Caro and Dad and head off to the bus stop.

This Marky boy better be good.

Chapter Fifteen

'He's not coming,' says Fran.

We've been standing under her pink sparkly umbrella outside the Central Line tube station for about fifteen minutes and there's no sign of Marky.

'Hmm?' I say in a distracted fashion.

I've drifted off into a sort of sad dream where I'm back with Sol.

Sol.

My scowling, olive-skinned First Love.

So far, anyway. I realise that life is quite long and I might have other boyfriends one day.

But I miss him. He made me feel small

and girlie and quite normal, like I didn't really have OCD.

How is it possible to miss someone you only knew for a few weeks?

The rain plops all over my feet and my denim jacket is damp at the sleeves.

People stream out of the tube station and huddle under umbrellas and deep inside coats.

It's not even like a real summer.

'Let's just go home,' I say to Fran. 'I think I'd rather watch Caro slice up her arms than stand here waiting for some bloke with a stupid "y" on the end of his name to turn up. Bet that wasn't even his real photo.'

There's a sort of coughing muttering noise behind me and I turn around to find a tall, handsome fair-haired boy gazing down at Fran.

'Zelah?' he says. 'Hi! I'm Marky.'

Fran stares up at this vision of gorgeousness with a smile beginning to spread over her face.

'She's not Zelah,' I say. 'I am. And feel free to look really disappointed.'

Marky has fantastic manners.

He turns away from Fran and holds out a hand to me.

Yikes. Major *Germ Alert*.

'She doesn't do handshaking,' says Fran, helpful as ever. 'She's got OCD.'

Nice one, Fran. Why not just get a huge flaming bomb and throw it into the middle of where we're standing?

Marky's grin fades just a little bit but he continues to smile down at me.

'OC what?' he says. 'Sorry. Don't know what that means.'

I want to say a lot of things at that moment.

I want to say, 'It means that my life is rubbish. It means that I can't even hug my own dad. It means that Heather, my next best thing to a mum, has to air-kiss me. It means that I

have to put sheets of paper on my chairs before my bottom touches their germ-encrusted cushions. It means that I spend a lot of time at the day care centre in the hospital. It means that I ended up in a weird home in Dorset where I met a bloke I really like but who's vanished off the face of the planet.'

But of course I don't say that 'cos Marky is still looking at me with that puzzled look in his blue eyes and Fran is still gazing at him with a faint flush on her smooth cheeks.

'Fran,' I say. 'Thanks for coming with. I'll be OK now. I'll text you later. OK?'

Fran gives Marky one last, lingering look and then backs away to the bus stop.

'Kebab?' I say. I don't even like kebabs but the area where we're standing has about fifteen kebab shops all in a line and I don't want to go too far – I just want to get this horrid moment over as soon as possible so that I can go home

and 'amuse' myself with Dad and Caro.

Marky glances up at the sign creaking back and forth over our head.

There's a faded drawing of a big brown kebab on it and a long streak of pigeon shit splattered across the front.

It says *Ali's Kebabs. Hot, tasty food while you wait.*

I don't understand how you'd get the food *without* waiting, but somehow it's just another confusing part of my crazy life.

'Lovely,' Marky says, opening the door for me.

A blast of hot, greasy, animal-entrails air sucks us both inside.

We sit in the corner next to two bald old men in leather waistcoats who are smoking something dodgy from a large glass bowl with a winding red tube coming out of it.

'I thought Shepherd's Bush was all full of television people and trendy clothes markets?' I say before I can stop myself.

'This bit isn't,' says Marky. 'But I live in the other bit. I've only come here because this is where you suggested that we meet.'

Fair enough.

'So,' says Marky when we're settled with two slimy kebabs flopping out of some limp pitta bread along with tiny shreds of wilted lettuce and watery tomato.

'Tell me what this OC thing is, then.'

I wrap my hand in a tissue so that I can pick up the horrid meat and to give myself a few extra seconds to work out a reply.

I don't know how to put it. The face opposite me isn't a face that will understand scrubbing and jumping and blood and counting and grease phobias and ducking to avoid bonfires.

The face opposite me kind of goes with healthy outdoor pursuits like tennis and swimming and sailing and horse riding.

Marky is VERY handsome. So handsome in fact that he doesn't look real.

I don't feel anything when I stare at him. Nothing at all. Well – perhaps a vague curiosity to know what product he uses on his skin 'cos it's amazing. But other than that, nothing.

I pick at my vile food for a moment and then I look him straight in the eye.

'It's kind of a control thing,' I say. 'Like if I don't do certain things, then other bad things might happen.'

'What sort of things?' says Marky, squirting what looks like the thick dark blood of a wild boar into his kebab and eating it with a pained expression on his ultra-tanned face.

'Well,' I say. 'Scrubbing is one of the things. I scrub my face thirty-one times on each cheek

in the morning and at bedtime and sometimes in the middle of the day if I'm stressed.'

'OK . . .' says Marky in a calm, polite sort of way but a hint of doubt has crept into his posh voice. 'So like it's an obsession thing?'

Now we're getting somewhere.

'Yes,' I say. 'It stands for "Obsessive Compulsive Disorder".'

Marky lights up like Oxford Street at Christmas when I say this.

'Hey, David Beckham's got that!' he says. He looks around in amazement as if expecting to see his football hero skulking in the corner of a kebab shop and dissecting a rank piece of dead meat into neat pieces. 'That's really cool, Zelah!' he says, biting with vigour into his kebab and ignoring the squirt of red ketchup that flies across the table and lands by my plate.

'Could you, like, mop that up, please?' I say.

'Or else I'm going to have to leave the table. That's another part of OCD. I don't like dirt.'

'Sure,' says Marky. He leans over and swipes the offending sauce away with a tissue and lobs it into a bin that's about half the shop away. 'Goal!' he shouts.

Honestly.

'So do you do that thing with the labels?' he continues. 'Only I was reading about how David Beckham has to line up all the cans in his cupboard so that they're facing the same way.'

'No, I'm not THAT bad,' I say, before I can stop myself. Actually I AM that bad – one glimpse into my ordered wardrobe would tell you that – but I don't line up the cans in our cupboard.

And even if I wanted to I couldn't.

Dad never buys any groceries so the only things in our food cupboard are stale Pot Noodles, some ancient orange-coloured stock

cubes and a jar of revolting poo-smelling gravy granules.

I couldn't touch them for fear of *Germ Alert* anyway so I'm never going to get to arrange all the labels to face forward.

Marky has finished his kebab and is staring at me with new fascination.

I'm trying to see my wristwatch under the table but it's too dark and poky in the kebab shop. All I can see is a bit of Marky's bony brown leg contrasting against his white tennis shorts.

He's still staring at me like I'm a rare hothouse plant stuck under a glass dome.

It's making me all fidgety and restless.

I don't want to go out with this boy so that he can show off to all his mates that he knows somebody who suffers from David Beckham Disease.

I want somebody to love me for being me.

Like Sol did. Or at least, if he didn't love me, he really, really liked me.

I want to be home with Dad and his vegetable patch.

Or even Caro. Gawd.

But at least Caro accepts me for who I am, OCD and all.

Marky is making a show of paying the bill for us both and sharing a hearty laugh with the kebab shop owner.

'Thanks, that was lovely,' I lie. I can already feel chewed-up bits of rancid lamb coming up into my mouth again.

'So – good luck with the dating,' I add as I make a rush for the door.

Marky pants along behind me as I leg it to the bus stop.

'Don't you want to see me again?' he says.

I can tell by this that he's not used to girls turning him down.

'I'm sure my friend Fran would love to,' I say. 'But I don't think that you and I are destined to be together.'

'Well, I'll wait with you until the bus comes,' he says, gallant to the last.

I roll my eyes when he can't see.

There's really no reason for him to hang about waiting with me.

'Marky' I say, all innocent. 'Why've you got a "y" on the end of your name?'

Marky smiles.

'It's just a nickname,' he says. 'When I was little my mother used to call me that. It kind of stuck.'

'Well, I hope you don't mind me saying,' I say. 'But I find it really annoying. What's wrong with just "Mark"?'

At that moment the bus sails into view and nearly knocks us off the kerb.

'I guess I just like to be a bit different,'

says Marky as I join the queue. 'Like you, Zelah. Your name's unusual. And you're certainly a bit different to most girls. But that's good, isn't it? I mean – being a bit different to everyone else.'

I reflect on this as I take my seat and wave Marky goodbye.

No, I think as the bus weaves its way back towards Acton.

I want to be just the same as everyone else.

Chapter Sixteen

After the date with Marky I get several more emails in the *mysortaspace.com* inbox but most of them seem to be from nutters and I'm considering closing down the account just to protect myself from further dating torture.

There's one from a boy called Stephen who sounds quite nice but then sends me his photo on email and he looks as if he might be about six so I bin that one straight away.

Then there's another one from a boy called Sim who sounds really keen and likes all the same bands I do, only then he sends through

his photograph and he looks about twenty-eight so I email back and mention that I'm training to be a policewoman when I leave school and it goes dead quiet after that.

And then there's someone who's obviously got a bit confused 'cos they turn out to be a GIRL.

'Hi,' it says. 'Boys are so dull. Fancy getting together for some Girl Action?'

I take action right away.

I press the 'delete' button. Hard.

Caro thinks that my dating adventures are hilarious.

'These dudes all sound shit,' she says, sparse as ever. 'Except maybe that guy with the Italian name. He sounds OK. If you don't want him, chuck him my way and I'll eat him with gravy for dinner.'

'Hang on,' I say. 'How do you know about

the guy with the Italian name?'

Caro tries to look ashamed but then she ruins it by smirking.

'Your password isn't exactly difficult to crack,' she says. ' I mean – "Zelah". Not very original, is it?'

I give her a faint smile. I'm getting used to having Caro around now. I've realised that much of what she says sounds rude and insulting but actually hides a shy and unhappy little person underneath.

And she's right in that Alessandro does sound kind of OK. Well – as OK as somebody you've never met can do, I s'pose. Which is why I said yes when he suggested that we meet up.

But I'm so tired and fed up with the entire summer holiday that I can't be bothered to dress up again in the long skirt and silver flip-flops and dangly earrings so when Saturday

comes around again I just get up, do my scrubs and jumps and put on jeans and a white T-shirt and a pair of plimsolls.

I brush my hair one hundred times on each side 'cos I'm stressed and it's raining again and I don't really want to go on the tube to Central London to meet Alessandro but that's where we've arranged to meet.

Fran turns up at ten and looks me up and down in despair.

'Zelah!' she says. 'You can't go on a date looking like you haven't made any effort!'

Fran is wearing a short flippy pink skirt, which flares out when she walks, pink flip-flops with diamond-studded edges and her best denim jacket. Her hair has been smoothed into two heavy plaits and tied at the ends with pink stretchy bands.

'Fran,' I say, looking at this vision of pinkness. 'You're such a – girl.'

Fran looks at her dainty pink watch and gasps.

'We've got to go!' she says. 'Quick – let me just do your hair.'

Standing in front of the hall mirror she performs wonders with my frizzy black bush of hair, tying it back into a pony. She takes off her gold hoop earrings with a tiny pink flower dangling from each and wipes them on a tissue. Then she inserts them into my ear lobes.

'Not as good as the other day,' she says. 'But you look better with the earrings in.'

We bolt out of the door for the tube.

Tube is gross.

I forgot how much the underground makes my OCD flare up.

There are greasy poles in the middle of the carriage and 'cos there's no room to sit down I'm standing right by one trying not to touch it

except that I have to or else I'd fall over on top of a load of horrid smelly unwashed bodies and die from *Germ Alert* and *Dirt Alert.*

Fran lets me grab on to the bell-shaped sleeves of her pink gypsy top instead when the train lurches to a stop in every station.

'Thanks,' I whisper.

I'm starting to get a gurgling sinking feeling of nerves in my stomach.

Yuk.

I hope this Alessandro bloke is worth it.

And more to the point, I hope he's clean.

Oxford Circus is this vile mass of moving, pushing, sweaty human bodies.

'Horrid,' I mutter as Fran pulls me by the sleeve up the escalator and then steers me out of the exit and into the harsh sunlight.

'Eughhh,' I say as we fight our way down Oxford Street towards the mega Topshop

on the other side of the road.

I keep hold of Fran's sleeve. People are rushing past me and bashing my elbows and bottom, which is major *Dirt Alert* AND *Germ Alert* so I do my 'phoo, phoo,' breaths to try and stay calm.

Not much chance of that.

There are so many people piling past us when we stand by the big concrete pillar outside Topshop that I go giddy.

A lot of boys smile at Fran, I notice.

She tosses her plaits and sticks her snub nose a fraction higher in the air. The only thing Fran's got her eye on is a sleeveless pink sundress modelled on a dummy as thin as a piece of cheese-wire.

I've told Alessandro that I've got frizzy black hair and will be standing outside Topshop with my beautiful ex-best friend who will probably be dressed in a lot of pink. I've said

that Fran's beautiful to avoid the awkward moment where his mouth gapes open and it's obvious to us both that he wishes he could go on a date with her instead.

Fran's peering across the road back towards the tube exit with a frown.

'That boy looks familiar,' she says.

I follow her gaze but it's difficult with all the other people jostling about in the middle of the road, dodging buses and taxis and hanging about in big untidy groups.

'Can't see a boy,' I mutter. I'm getting grumpy and hot.

'There,' says Fran, pointing.

I can see the tip of somebody's head but that's about it.

'I'm sure I *know* him,' says Fran. 'Oh well – it can't be Alessandro anyway. He's late, by the way.'

She glances behind us at the window of

Topshop again. I can practically hear the money screaming to get out of her purse and into the cash till.

'Sorry,' I say. 'I'm getting a bit fed up waiting as well.'

I turn around and look into the window of Topshop at a pair of silver flip-flops a bit like mine but with a big white daisy stuck on the front.

Hmm. Nice.

I'm just wondering whether I should give up the whole dating thing and go shopping with Fran instead when I realise that she's talking to somebody.

'I *knew* I recognised you!' she's saying. 'Weird! I mean – I only met you that once.'

I turn round with a scowl, prepared to tell Fran to stop chatting up strangers and concentrate on the matter at hand – me.

I smell him before I see him.

Shower gel.

Deodorant.

Faint whiff of tobacco.

'Hi, Zelah,' says a gruff voice.

Topshop starts collapsing behind me and I fall against the concrete pillar for support.

Dirt Alert fades into the background. I try to prop myself up, make some words come out of my mouth.

But all I can manage is:

'Y–you!'

Chapter Seventeen

He's sort of grinning at me, all shaved head and light olive skin.

His dark eyes are shining with amusement.

'Sol,' I manage. 'What are you doing here?'

'Same as you two,' says Sol. He's grinning like a demented alley cat now.

'What – staring at dresses in Topshop?' I say.

Fran is looking from me to Sol and back again. Some sort of light has been switched on in her face.

'Oh, I get it!' she says.

'I wish I did,' I say. 'Get what? We're here

because I'm supposed to be going on a blind date, by the way. But the stupid idiot never turned up.'

'Zelah,' hisses Fran. 'Haven't you switched your brain on today?'

I continue to stare at Sol and then at Fran and then around the area outside Topshop just in case my blind date is standing there all lonely and ignored.

Sol is laughing now. Proper loud laughing, not the quiet shoulder-shaking sort he used to do at Forest Hill.

'Zelah,' he says. 'I am that stupid idiot.'

He and Fran fall about while I try to pick my brains off the floor where they've been trampled by sale shoppers.

'But,' I start. This is way too weird. 'But – I'm supposed to be meeting somebody called "Alessandro".'

'And?' says Sol. 'Here I am.'

Fran gives me a virtual shoulder-pat, a big grin, and then rushes into Topshop with a purposeful glint in her eye.

'See you here at five!' she yells as she sinks down on a crowded escalator into the bowels of the shop.

I watch the top of her shiny head until it disappears, just to give me time to find some words.

Sol is still grinning.

'You weren't very hard to track down,' he says. 'I mean – Zelah! You can't use your own name on a networking site when it's that unusual!'

I draw myself up from the pillar and give him a hard stare.

'Well, at least I'm not hiding behind a fake name,' I say. 'I mean – Alessandro! What's that all about? Sounds like a creepy waiter in an Italian restaurant!'

Sol's turn to look aggrieved now.

'Actually, that's my real name,' he says. 'But I've always been known as "Sol" at home.'

There's a short silence during which I become aware that I want a big hole to appear and swallow me up, that my hands need a good wash and that my throat has dried to cinder toast.

Sol sees me looking down at my fingers.

'Still got the OCD, yeah?' he says in a softer voice.

I nod. Can't speak for a moment.

Memories of Forest Hill come flooding back.

The first time he opened up to me about his mum dying and his father going to pieces.

The last time I saw him out of the back of the car window as Dad and Heather drove me home.

'Your dad!' I say, remembering the email I

had last week. 'How did he end up in prison?'

Sol sighs.

He looks around and then gestures towards a cafe down a side street on the other side of the road.

'Let's go and grab a drink,' he says. 'I'll fill you in.'

We walk down Oxford Street in silence. Not touching, of course. That would be major *Germ Alert* and *Dirt Alert*.

But close.

Chapter Eighteen

It's been three months since I last saw Sol at Forest Hill.

I study him across the table in the cafe while he glances down the menu.

He looks better than he did then.

His face has filled out, even though his cheekbones are still to die for.

He smiles a lot more.

And most amazing of all, he talks in great non-stop streams of speech.

'Wow,' I say after he's put in an order for tea, coffee, cake, biscuits and beans on toast. 'You've gone the opposite way. Now you won't shut up!'

Sol flashes me one of his dazzling grins and settles back in his orange plastic chair.

'So,' he says. 'I was surfing the net and I just kind of wondered how you might be doing. Typed in your name and went right to that website. The rest was pretty easy.'

I'm racking my brains to see if I said anything embarrassing in my emails to the bloke I thought was 'Alessandro' but I can't think of much at all with him sitting there grinning.

Real live Sol. Sitting there in front of me.

About thirty plates of food turn up on our table.

I pull out my own knife and fork from the pocket of Fran's jacket and inspect all the plates to make sure there's no specks of dirt or crumbs where there shouldn't be.

Sol watches me, his dark eyes scowling under heavy brows.

'I thought maybe Forest Hill had sorted you out,' he says.

I pick up a piece of toast in a white napkin, inspect it for any foreign bodies, check the underside twice and bring it gingerly to my lips.

'Kind of. A bit,' I say. 'I've cut down my jumping and scrubbing. But it's been a bad summer.'

'Oh yeah,' says Sol. 'You mentioned that you've got Caro staying with you. Nightmare. How come?'

I explain how she just turned up on my doorstep like a lost satanist and Sol laughs in a fearful way.

'Good luck with that,' is all he says, but his eyes sparkle.

Then he demolishes a big plate of beans and stuffs in a couple of cakes.

I wait until he's finished 'cos I quite like gazing at his smooth shaved head while he's

eating and then I ask him about his dad.

Sol wipes his mouth and leans back in his chair again.

'It was good for a while, yeah?' he says. 'I went back to live with Dad for a few weeks. He made like a really big effort. He was amazed that I could talk again. Then we started to talk about what happened to Mum. That was when he sort of started going to pieces.'

I nod. I remember Sol telling me about his parents.

'Then what?' I say, peeling a cake out of a white wrapper with a tissue clamped to my hand.

'Then he started staying out later and later,' says Sol. 'And one night he didn't come home. I rang the police and they said they'd arrested him for burglary. That was the last time I saw him out of prison.'

'Oh,' I say. I can feel my eyes going all

watery. Sol all abandoned and orphan-like, with a mother dead and a father locked up.

He gives a brief laugh and mops a piece of bread around what's left of his bean plate.

'You don't need to feel sorry for me,' he says. 'I've moved in with my granddad in East London. It's cool. We get on kind of OK. He's got a girlfriend who's ten years younger than him.'

I nod.

'Hey, what's this about playing in a heavy metal band,' I say, remembering the emails. 'Maybe you should be going out with Caro.'

Sol shudders. 'That girl,' he says, 'is related to the Antichrist. Anyway, she's more goth than slash metal really.'

'Oh, right,' I say. I don't know much about either goth or metal apart from the weird noises I hear coming from Caro's bedroom.

Sol tells me about his band and the songs

he's been writing and then it's nearly five o'clock already so he pays the bill and we head back into the street in silence.

There's no sign of Fran outside Topshop yet but then again she tends to lose track of time when surrounded by shoes and dresses so me and Sol stand back by the concrete pillar and he moves into my Personal Space which I always kind of need as it's how I avoid *Germ Alert* and *Dirt Alert* and the thing is I kind of don't mind because it's Sol and he makes my heart thump faster but then another little voice in me is screaming in panic 'cos it looks as if he might DO something any moment and I kind of wish Fran would come back but half-wish that she'd get lost forever in the changing rooms of Topshop and I'm obviously looking a bit hot and flustered because Sol changes from moving towards me to kind of stepping back and nearly crashing into a group of girl

tourists hanging about looking at maps behind him.

'Sorry,' he says. I'm not sure whether he's saying it to me or to the girls so I give a kind of half-smile.

'Erm, don't suppose I could hold your hand for a moment?' he says, all hopeful.

He bends his head a bit closer. I can smell the shower gel again.

The last time I saw Sol at Forest Hill he held my hand. It was only for a couple of seconds but it was the first time I'd touched somebody on their skin for over two years.

I can still remember what it felt like. Dry, warm, *alive*.

Scary. But amazing too.

I look down at my hands

Then I start holding one out towards Sol but the hand develops a will of its own and dives back into my pocket again.

'Sorry, sorry,' I say. I want to die.

I want to be rid of my OCD so badly that my guts twist and ache.

'It's OK,' says Sol, but it isn't really.

We stand there like two awkward strangers at a bus stop, shifting from one foot to another and raising our eyebrows and saying 'Well,' and 'Hmm . . .' and 'So!' a few times until I think I'm going to expire with embarrassment and then Fran's there again with a big handful of rustling bags and Sol is grinning at her and making some feeble joke about saving the environment and then the next thing I'm back on the tube with Fran and she's gazing at me with big concerned eyes.

We only speak about two words all the way home even though she's bought me the silver flip-flops with the big flowers on which is really sweet.

I want to get home and lie on the bed and cry for England.

I want my OCD to go away.

Chapter Nineteen

All over the rest of the weekend I check my email about a zillion times but there's nothing from Sol although there are some nice texts from Fran asking if I'm OK.

Somehow I didn't really think that there would be.

I'm too screwed-up for him now. He's sorted out his life and got on top of his non-talking problem.

And I'm still scrubbing at my cheeks with a nail brush loaded up with harsh white soap and I'm still jumping until my feet get sore and I've even developed a new symptom which

involves tapping ten times on the end of the banister before I do my jumps or else I've convinced myself that Heather will die in Slovenia and never come home to rescue me from this horrible school holiday.

I probably looked like a hopeless case to Sol.

Wouldn't blame him if he never got in touch again.

Monday.

Caro gets up late but then goes out, refusing to tell me where she's going.

She comes back from wherever she's been at the same time Dad arrives home from school.

She's got a look on her face that I recognise.

It's kind of smirking and self-important and superior and mysterious all at the same time.

It's the same look she used to get just

before she teased Alice or Lib at Forest Hill House with some devastating insult that would have Alice in floods of tears or Lib speechless with anger.

'What?' I snap. I am not in the mood for Caro's nastiness.

And now Dad's come home looking a little red around the eyes. Again. He's bought us a Chinese takeaway as a treat but I can't help looking at his eyes and wishing that Heather would come back and stop him visiting the pub after work.

Dad's missing Heather a lot. He won't admit it, but I've caught him gazing at her photograph all moony-eyed and pathetic when he thinks I've gone to bed.

He's pining and lovesick.

Maybe that's why he has a drink every day after work.

I decide to try and be more understanding.

'Do any of the other teachers go to the pub with you?' I say.

Dad is tipping a bag of prawn crackers into a big glass bowl. He stops mid-pour at that but then carries on, his back to me.

Caro sniggers.

Just a tiny sound, but it's enough to wind me up.

'Could you just manage to stay out of the conversation for once, please?' I say.

She makes a mock-scared face at me and dives into a carton of noodles before anybody else has a chance to sit down, sucking them up with her eyes crossed and bits of chopped chicken dripping down her chin.

'Gross,' I say. 'Anyway, Dad. You were saying?'

Dad comes to join us at the table.

He snaps open a can of lager, even though he's just been to the pub.

Caro catches my eye and gives me that odd, knowing little smile again.

I am going to ignore the can of lager.

'Yes, one or two other teachers go,' says Dad. 'Prawn balls, anyone?'

Caro leans over and helps herself to more than half the container.

I reach over to her plate and take some back.

It's about time that Caro learned some manners, I reckon.

'Ooh, OCD's got a cob on!' says Caro. 'She'd be even crosser if she knew what I know!'

I ignore her. I dip my clean spoon into one of the containers and then a different clean spoon into each box. That way I avoid the risk of major *Germ Alert*.

Caro's not going to let it drop.

'I said, you'd be really angry if you knew what I know,' she says, louder this time.

Dad's got his head down and is wolfing

down food very fast without looking up.

I swear I see him kick Caro's leg underneath the table. Hard.

I decide I'll pretend I haven't seen the kick or heard what Caro is trying to tell me.

'Why are prawn crackers so moreish, do you think?' I say. My voice is high and a bit hysterical.

Caro gives her evil little laugh again.

'Dunno,' she says. 'Why is *lager* so moreish, do you reckon? What makes people drink so much of it?'

Dad gets up, having eaten his meal in record time, and fills up the kettle.

There's a very odd feeling in the air. Like summer has finished early and autumn is about to lower one hell of a frost over the house and garden.

'Well?' says Caro. 'Isn't anybody going to answer my question?'

I've had enough of this and I'm in a foul mood anyway because of the whole dating disaster with Sol.

'Caro,' I say. 'Dad's bought us a really nice dinner. You're being rude. I don't know why you're being rude but then again I never do. Can't you just button it for one short evening?'

Caro gets up and shoves back her chair. Her smile has gone. She grabs a carton of rice and makes for the kitchen door.

'Don't you dare have a go at me,' she spits. 'It's not me you need to be angry with. Maybe you need to ask your precious father here what he's doing every day when you think he's being a schoolteacher.'

I feel the colour drain from my face.

Dad slinks out of the room and goes up to his study.

'What do you mean?' I say. My legs have

gone all shaky and I have a strong urge to run upstairs and scrub my hands until they are red raw.

'I saw him!' says Caro. Her voice is loaded with satisfaction. 'Your precious dad. I saw him in the pub this afternoon at two o'clock. And I bet you that's where he's been every day this week.'

She slams out of the room so hard that the clock falls off the wall and smashes into shards of black and white at my feet.

I stand there for ages like a pale zombie.

My feet are rooted to the floor.

I can't move because I'm frozen with fear.

Caro's many things, but she's not a liar.

And Dad?

He's been lying to me all along.

Chapter Twenty

Dad doesn't stay upstairs for long.

He comes downstairs dragging Caro by the wrist.

For once she's lost that smug look. Her eyes are full of fear.

'Sit down,' he says. He pushes her into a chair.

I'm still standing frozen in the middle of the room.

'You too, Zelah,' he says.

I manage to get myself to a chair. I can't look Dad in the eye.

'Before you start on me,' he says, 'yes, it's

true. I haven't been going to my new job. I've been sitting in the pub all day. I can't deny it.'

I'm speechless with disappointment. All that time trying to keep Dad's spirits lifted, the trip to buy new clothes, the phone calls to Heather and how proud she was of Dad getting a new teaching job.

'Zelah,' he says. 'Say something. Anything. But don't sit there in silence. I feel terrible enough about this as it is.'

Caro's never silent for long, though.

'God, how pathetic,' she says. 'Pretending to your own daughter that you're going to work when all the time you're holed up in the local boozer being a sad old lush.'

Dad turns his head towards Caro.

For the first time in years I see real anger in his eyes.

'I opened up my home to you,' he says. 'I've taken you in and let you live here rent-

free and how have you paid me in return?'

I don't think Dad actually expects an answer to this question but Caro being Caro is going to give him one anyway.

'Been a charming and fun lodger, not like your own miserable screwed-up daughter?' she says.

I glare at her.

'Zelah's worth a hundred of you,' says Dad.

'Zelah's a freak,' continues Caro, not to be outdone. 'Come on, man. We both know it.'

My father stands up and looms over her, a tower of red rage in his checked shirt and with his watery pink-rimmed eyes.

'Enough,' he says. His voice is like reinforced steel.

'I'd like you to leave our house, as of now,' he continues.

Caro's expression of superiority begins to fade away.

'What? I can't . . . you know I can't,' she stutters. 'Where will I go?'

Dad flaps his hands at her as if he is dismissing her from his life forever. Which he probably is.

'You should have thought of that,' he says. 'You'll go back to the decent foster parents who, for some reason unknown to mankind, have taken it upon themselves to give you a good home.'

Caro opens up her black-lipsticked mouth and lets out a scream of rage.

I've heard that scream a few times before but it never fails to make all the hairs on my body stand to attention. It's the sort of scream I would make if somebody sliced open my soft white abdomen with a carving knife that hadn't been disinfected.

Dad looks taken aback for a moment but continues to stand over Caro with a

threatening expression.

'Go and pack,' he says. 'I'm ringing your foster parents. They can come and get you or you can hitch back the way you came. I'm past caring.'

Caro's gone purple with rage now. She looks around the kitchen with a wild expression on her face.

Her gaze settles on the back garden and I know in a split second what she's going do and I shout out 'NO, CARO!' but it's too late and like a black flash of spite she's off out of the kitchen door and down the end of the garden and heading straight for the spade that Dad leaves stuck in the flower bed at the end of a long day's gardening.

Dad and I follow but it's too late.

With shrieks of rage and grunts of effort Caro attacks all the lines of neat vegetables with the spade, sending a flurry of green leaves

flying up into the air. Then with her hands she rips down the beautiful cane pyramids which prop up the red bean flowers until they are bent and snapped and all tangled up with the earthy roots lying on the grass.

'STOP IT!' I scream as I rush towards her. 'CARO! STOP!'

Yes. It's way too late now.

Caro raises the handle of the heavy spade in the direction of Dad's beloved greenhouse with its neat rows of grapes and new tomatoes hanging in little jewel-like clusters and with one scream of effort she's smashed all the glass into tiny crystals and swiped all the plastic seed trays and their contents on to the floor.

I run into the greenhouse and try to wrestle the spade out of her surprisingly strong grip. For a small thin person Caro seems to possess supernatural powers. Earth and bits of dried wood and weed fall all over me but I'm too

stressed to register the *Dirt Alert*.

I pull and tug at the spade but Caro's stronger than I am.

Then another pair of hands reaches in and grabs it.

Dad.

I think he's going to put the spade out of Caro's reach but what he does next catches all of us unawares.

He looms over Caro with the spade still in his grasp.

And lets out an enormous roar.

Chapter Twenty-One

There's a horrid sickening moment of slow motion where I see Caro cowering in fright and my father looming over her like a whale of wrath and now I'm moving towards Dad to try and stop him.

'You little cow!' Dad is shouting. 'You vile, evil child!' I snap out of slow motion and get myself positioned between Caro and the spade.

'No, Dad!' I say. 'You can't hit her!'

I never told my dad much about Caro's past. About the father who used to hit and abuse her up in her bedroom when she was

just a tiny child. About how her self-harming is all because of the fear she used to feel as a little girl.

My dad is ashen with shock when he hears my voice.

He drops the spade and stands there, a broken man with tears pouring down his face.

Caro's also crying. It's a quiet whimper of fear, like an animal that's just been kicked.

When Dad drops the spade she dodges his bulk and darts out of the greenhouse and back towards the house.

The garden looks like a wilderness.

All Dad's orderly lines of vegetables have gone.

The neat grass is strewn with lumps of soil and the leaves of ripped-up plants.

The wooden bean-frames lie drunkenly on their sides or sticking up towards the sky like the crushed limbs of giant stick insects.

Dad drops to his knees and buries his face in his hands.

Great big sobs come from his shaking body.

It's at that moment that I stop seeing Dad as a weak, unemployed, lovesick drinking man.

He's a human being. In pain. Lots of.

I crouch down next to him and I'm kneeling in piles of compost and earth and manure and other shit but I don't care.

For the first time in over three years I reach out and touch my dad.

I put my arms around him and he gives a little jolt of surprise but I hang on for grim death even though my whole body is screaming *DIRT ALERT!* and *GERM ALERT!* at me in the loudest voice you've ever heard.

I hold on for ages and then another

thought enters my head.

Caro. Where's she gone?

I leg it back towards the house at top speed.

Chapter Twenty-Two

She's not in her room.

I look around upstairs, shouting out her name, but there's no reply.

Her clothes are all still in the wardrobe but there's no sign of the girl.

'CARO!' I yell as I run back downstairs to check the lounge and kitchen.

She's not there.

I take a moment to breathe deep and slow, just like the Doc showed me.

'Phoo, phoo,' I go, leaning against the kitchen door.

Then I see it.

The hook where we keep the key and the spare key to Heather's house.

It's empty.

In a flash I'm up the path and hammering on Heather's front door without even thinking about the contact between my hand and the wood.

'CARO,' I call through the letterbox. 'LET ME IN!'

There's no sound.

'Oh, gawd,' I say. I've left Dad all traumatised in the garden too.

I go round the back of Heather's house and peer in all the windows and rattle the back door but everything is locked.

I'm thinking that maybe I should call the police so I run home and grab my mobile but in the end I do a weird thing.

I call Fran.

And within ten minutes of my garbled

phone call she comes skidding down the road on her mountain bike with her plaits flying out behind her.

'What is it?' she pants. I'd only had breath to sob 'Emergency!' into the phone.

I explain about Dad and Caro and Caro's dodgy past.

Fran turns white.

'We have to break in,' she says, ignoring my squeak of protest. 'Heather would understand. This is a matter of life and death.'

I'd forgotten how good Fran was in a crisis.

A moment later she's broken the kitchen window at the back with a brick wrapped in a handkerchief and she's feeling around for the catch and we're both climbing through the window and falling into the sink in a tangle of arms and legs.

'Eughhh,' I say. There's cold water in the sink and I've landed right in it.

'Zelah, never mind the water,' snaps Fran. 'Let's find your friend.'

'She's not my friend,' I start to say. Then I stop.

I'm worried about Caro, more worried than I've ever been about anyone.

So maybe she *is* my friend. Sort of. Although she treats me like crap.

Fran has bolted up the stairs ahead of me.

'FOUND HER!' she calls down.

I hear her pick up Heather's phone and dial a number.

'Ambulance, please,' she says in her calm, grown-up voice.

My heart thumps as I race upstairs.

Caro's lying across Heather's bed.

The duvet is usually a pristine white but today it seems to have bright red poppies all over it.

At least that's what I think.

Then I realise what's happening.

The whole world goes black and fuzzy.

Everyone disappears.

Chapter Twenty-Three

When I wake up I'm back home again and lying on Mum's side of the bed upstairs and there's a woman in a green outfit shining a torch into my eyes.

'She's fine,' says the woman. 'Probably just the shock.'

'No, it was the blood,' says Fran's voice. She's sitting on the opposite side of the bed.

'I'm not good with blood,' I say. My mouth is all dry and tastes rank.

'She's not good with blood,' says Fran. 'She's got OCD.'

OK, OK. No need to labour the point.

'Where's Caro?' I say, sitting up in a panic.

I see her as she was a few moments ago, lying pale and limp across the duvet with her wrists leaking blood and a sheen of grey sweat on her pretty-evil face.

'She's gone to hospital,' says the woman in green.

'She'll be OK,' says Dad, who's standing at the foot of the bed. 'I'm so sorry I got angry with her. I'd forgotten what you told me about her family history. Not that I'm making excuses for what I did.'

I reach out and do something I couldn't do with Sol the other day.

I hold Dad's hand. Because I haven't done much hand-holding since I was twelve, it feels really weird. I can feel the wrinkles over his knuckles and the hairs on his fingers and the rough texture of his palms.

'Wow,' says Dad. 'You do realise you're

actually holding my hand, Princess?'

He wipes away a tear.

Fran gives me a big smile, a real one.

'I'm glad you're OK and that Caro is safe in hospital,' she says.

Then before I can find the words to reply she's off downstairs and away down the street on her bike.

'Something I've got to do,' she calls on the way out.

Dad and I look at one another. Dad is all covered in mud, earth, grass and plants and he looks broken, like an older version of the same man.

'Sorry I let you down,' he says, but it's enough.

I give him my own version of the smile Fran just gave me.

He is my dad, after all.

Chapter Twenty-Four

The day after Caro's admission to hospital the house feels really quiet and strange and calm.

Dad and I tiptoe around one another being apologetic and helpful and trying to smile.

To my utter amazement I begin to miss having Caro around. I miss her horrid music and her vile way of verbally attacking me. I miss the way she puts her boots up on the table and rolls her fags. I even miss her bad moods and her door-slamming, chair-tipping tantrums.

'I must be going mental,' I say to myself.

'On top of my little problem. Oh great.'

It's now three days after she left and I'm combing my hair so hard it's nearly falling out.

Dad's outside trying to fix all the damage Caro did. He's raided Heather's emergency cash box and ordered a man to come and put new glass in the greenhouse and he's planted a load more seeds which he says should be up in time for late autumn as long as no more plant-destroying maniacs go at them with a spade.

I do thirty more brushes on the right hand side of my head, thirty on the left and thirty on the back.

I tie my hair back into a neat ponytail and take a long skirt from the wardrobe.

Then I have to move all the other items hanging nearby so that the gaps in between each item measure an exact four centimetres. I cave in and use a ruler for the second time this week.

I hunt about for flip-flops and go downstairs.

Fifty jumps on the top step today and fifty on the bottom and then for some reason I have to do fifty in the kitchen before I can allow myself to eat breakfast.

I sit at the table all on my own with a bowl of Rice Krispies and I listen to the little grains of rice as they pop and crackle and I think:

Other than Fran, Rice Krispies might be my only friends in the world.

That's one heck of a sad thought.

I've got nearly three weeks of summer holiday left. My father is still unemployed and depressed, my ex-best friend is being much nicer to me but we've still got a long way to go, the love of my life has reappeared and then faded out of my life again and my Antichrist friend, Caro, is in Somerset, where I'd like to be too if only I didn't have Dad to look after

and about a million bits of homework.

I feel sad and tired and deflated.

'I can't see an end to this,' I say out loud just as Dad comes in through the open kitchen door.

'End to what?' says Dad in a high posh fashion-editor sort of a voice.

The smell of Chanel perfume floods the kitchen.

I'm up out of my chair before you can say 'Slovenia'.

Heather's beaming from ear to ear.

'Surprised?' she says.

'Yes, very!' I say.

Dad is still down the bottom of the garden.

He's going to be even more surprised. And bowled over by pathetic old-person love, I expect.

'Why have you come back so early?' I say.

Heather's tipping out bottles of perfume and packets of chocolate from duty-free bags all over the kitchen table.

'Oh, you know,' she says. 'Too much champagne wrecks the complexion, kiddo. Remember that.'

Heather's a terrible liar.

'You know something, don't you?'

Heather stops squirting herself from bottles and tries to put on an innocent expression but it doesn't work.

'OK,' she says. 'Your friend Fran rang me up. She's a good kid, you know. She was really worried about your OCD.'

I let these words sink in. Fran. Fran was worried about me. Just like the old Fran before all the doubts got in the way.

I realise something at that moment.

I realise that just because you fall out with

222

your best friend and you feel like killing each other, it doesn't mean that some small seed of that friendship won't somehow survive and start to grow all over again.

I smile a real smile for the first time in ages.

I'm going to give Marky's telephone number to Fran as a thank you.

'She told me,' says Heather in a more stern tone of voice, 'that your dad stopped going to his new job. Is this true?'

I shift about in my chair and look out at Dad.

'Erm, yes, sort of, a bit,' I say.

Heather is aghast.

'You poor, poor child!' she says. 'You're far too young to be worrying about all this stuff! Honestly, Zelah, I feel awful!'

I tell Heather about Caro's moment of vegetable-rage and she gasps and looks

shocked and covers her mouth and then tries
not to laugh.

'Oh Zelah,' she says. 'What a summer
holiday you've had! Or not had, to be more
precise.'

'There's more,' I say.

I relate the tragic tale of how I met up with
Sol outside Topshop.

Heather's eyes grow as big as beetroots as I
move on to the bit about not being able to
hold his hand.

'I should have been here for you,' she says.
'I could have given you some moral support or
got you a fabulous deal on a designer dress.'

Then she presents me with a weird stuffed
Slovenian teddy bear and marches off down
the garden towards Dad with a purposeful
glint in her eye.

It's the final week of my holidays and at last

it feels like I am doing what I'm supposed to be doing.

A Big Fat Nothing.

And guess what?

I've just logged on all reluctant and sad and I've got an email from Sol!

This is what it says:

Dear Zelah, hope you're OK. It was fun seeing you again the other day even though I could see it was a bit stressful for you. Sorry about that. But maybe we could meet up in town again some day? Love, Sol. P.S. You looked kind of hot.

Now I'm in a dilemma. I don't know whether he means 'hot' as in sexy or 'hot' as in I was all flushed and bothered because I wasn't expecting him to turn up or try to hold my hand.

Hmm. But at least the email doesn't tell me to get lost.

Things are better at home too.

Heather's taken control of Dad. He's got another interview lined up and this time she's determined that he will get the job and stay in it. For a Very Long Time.

So I haven't got too much to worry about.

Even my rituals have got a bit better now. I've cut down my jumps again to fifteen and I've reduced the number of times I scrub my face and hands to twenty.

So, I'm lying up in my bedroom staring at the ceiling with nothing much to do and the sun's out and Dad and Heather are chatting away downstairs and I've caught up on all my homework and the phone rings and I'm nearest so I pick it up.

'Hi,' says Caro's voice. It sounds wary and older.

'Hi,' I say after a short pause. 'How are you?'

'Back at Forest Hill,' says Caro. 'The Doc drove over and got me from the hospital.'

I swallow hard. I hope Caro's not going to lay into me again. Just when everything was calming down and getting better.

'Don't start,' I say. 'I'm not sure I could stand it. I've cut down my jumps.'

'Chill, OCD,' says the familiar voice. 'You get yourself worked up, don't you? I'm not ringing to have a go.'

That takes the wind out of my sails.

'Oh,' is all I can manage. For a moment I wonder if this is some imposter pretending to be Caro.

'Yeah, I was ringing to say something else,' says Caro. 'Bear with me. This is not going to be easy, man.'

I brace myself for the insult or the revelation or the unwelcome news.

But it never comes.

'Thanks, Zelah,' is all that Caro says in a voice I've never heard before. 'Thanks for

putting up with me. And say thanks to your dad, and that.'

There's a gentle click.

She's gone.

Wow. Caro said something kind! It's a miracle!

I look at myself in the mirror. I see a happy sunburned girl with frizzy black hair and red cheeks.

Maybe the summer just got a whole lot better.

I'm galloping downstairs after doing only ten jumps on the top step and I've just reached the bottom one and am about to do the same and then burst into the kitchen except that Heather and Dad are speaking about something in very low voices and obviously don't want me to hear, so I stand very still and try to eavesdrop, but I can't really hear anything although I *swear* at one point I might have heard the word

'wedding' but that can't be right.

Heather will never agree to marry Dad.

Probably just as well.

I mean – all that worry, and organisation, and stress and planning!

Heather's way too busy with work to organise a wedding. And Dad would be useless at anything involving fashion and women and crying.

So – I wonder who'd have to deal with all *that?*

No! They wouldn't – they *couldn't* . . . not after my dreadful summer.

I shake my head and dismiss the thought.

I do ten very quiet jumps on the bottom stair.

Then I go to join my family.

Acknowledgements

Thanks to Leah Thaxton and the team at Egmont for their enthusiasm on all things Zelah-related. As ever Peter Buckman has remained the eternal optimist and been wonderfully candid and encouraging, so special thanks to him and all at The Ampersand Agency. And writing wouldn't be possible without the love and support of David, Carol and Tim Curtis, Tim Cowin and my lovely friend Sue Fox.

Also by Vanessa Curtis:

Zelah ♡ Green

'My name is Zelah Green and I'm a cleanaholic.'

I spend most of my life running away from germs. And dirt. And people. And I'm just about doing OK and then my stepmother packs me off to some kind of hospital to live with a load of strangers. It's stuck in the middle of nowhere. *Great.*

There's Alice who's anorexic. Caro who cuts herself. Silent Sol who has the cutest smile. And then there's me.

'It'll be fine, I say to myself. It's all going to be OK ...'

ZeLaH ♡ GReen

One More
Little Problem